KATE WARNE

PINKERTON'S FIRST LADY

UNITED STATES FIRST FEMALE DETECTIVE

By: **John Derrig**

SPIDER BOOKS
PUBLISHING

Pinkerton's First Lady–Kate Warne
United States' First Female Detective

Copyright © 2014 by John Derrig

Spider Books Publishing
2968 Ribbon Ct
Ft Myers FL 33905
SpiderBooksPublishing.com

ISBN: 978-0-9916538-1-2 (Print)
ISBN: 978-1-942728-31-3 (Digital)

Cover design, story development, & book layout by
Jennifer FitzGerald
MotherSpider.com.
Edited by Mother Spider Publishing

Excerpts from Erik Lerner

Remembrance of Kate Warne written by Roger Wright

Dedication

To my family: my wife Doris M. Derrig, my daughter Candice M. Derrig-Petaccio and son-in-law Jason and his mother Pat. My son John D. Derrig and daughter-in-law Ashley Derrig, my granddaughters Ariana and Alyssa Petaccio, Aubray Derrig, and my sister-Donna Derrig-Foote.

Thank you for being a good representation of a Law Enforcement family, who were all a great inspiration for this book. I love you all.

Table of Contents

Chapter I

1856-The Scene

"I'll be off now, Darling!" the man called out as he took his hat off the coat rack and started through the door. He walked down the hall to the stairwell that led to the apartment building's entrance.

"G'morning," he said to his neighbor, tipping his hat slightly and pressing his back against the wall to allow the elderly woman enough room to pass. The building's halls were relatively small, and he was obstructed by another tenant of the building as he made his way to the stairs.

"G'morning," he said, as again he tipped his hat. When he finally made it to the stairs, he checked his jacket for lint and wiped away any dandruff, then walked out the door, closed it behind him and took a deep breath before he began his journey.

It was a hot Wednesday and the time was high noon; the city was a heat trap. Between the buildings, the horse-drawn carriages, and the immense number of civilians

occupying the sidewalks and roads, it was like walking around in a large, low-burning furnace. As soon as he crossed the street, he entered the hustle and bustle of the great city of Chicago. To his right was a woman hanging out of a second floor window, beating a carpet on the side of the building. Below her, on the first floor of this block-long building, was a general store.

"If I'm not mistaken, her husband, Norman, owns that store; I wonder where he's run off to. It's not like him to open the store late," the man thought to himself as he continued down the sidewalk and observed the city around him. He enjoyed going on these types of walks, and his jovial expression reflected that joy.

He walked about three more blocks and passed a slaughter house, a fresh food stand, women fanning themselves, and several men who were shouting at everyone to buy their goods. He walked up to his favorite local bar and opened the door. He walked inside, took off his hat, and checked the time on his pocket watch. It was 12:35 in the afternoon.

"Philip!" the man behind the bar counter exclaimed.

"Edgar," Philip said as he wiped the sweat from his forehead.

"I hardly recognized you, you goosecap. Look at you. I must say you clean up very well for a washed up copper." Edgar responded.

Philip walked up to the counter and sat on a stool. He put his hat on the counter and rubbed his eyes. "I'm not a washed up copper, Ed. Don't call me a copper either, before you force me to give you a blinker."

Edgar leaned over and pulled out two small shot glasses and placed them on the counter. "Come, flicker with me."

"It's too early, I have to work soon anyway," Philip said.

Edgar took one of the two glasses and put it back under the counter. "Well I hope you don't mind if I indulge."

Philip turned his head and waved his hand to signify that he didn't care. Edgar nodded and poured himself a shot of whiskey and drank it.

"So," he asked Philip, "What's the job for today? You on the prowl for more sneeze-lurkers?" Edgar gave a loud laugh and stared at Philip with a grin. Philip gave him a stern look as though he were condemning him with his eyes. However, he knew that to some his profession seemed to be a joke.

Philip leaned back and scratched the side of his face. "I know that my line of work seems to be a joke to you, but with all these lushingtons having their choice in which groggery to go to and then robbing people on the streets afterwards, Chicago needs a few detectives out in the city. No more corrupt copper stations that take bribes, or are filled with whoremongers that the police ignore when they're not servicing them. I can arrest more scalawags on my own than

Some slang from the time: Goosecap is a silly fellow, sneeze-lurker is a thief who throws snuff in a person's face and then robs them, and as you might guess, a lushington is a drunk and a groggery is a bar.

a copper at a station could. I'm meeting someone."

Philip then pulled out his pocket watch and checked the time again, it was 12:46. He looked over his left shoulder to the entrance of the diner.

"So when should he be here?" Edgar asked, as he began pouring another shot of whiskey.

"He should have been here by now. To tell you the truth I was actually late," Philip answered as he turned back around and put his pocket watch back into his vest.

"So friend, shall I pour you up a horn of old orchard?"

Edgar took the second shot glass from under counter and placed it in front of Philip. Philip tapped the counter twice with his index finger. Edgar filled both glasses and they drank together.

"This is a lonely job," said Philip, "but I love what I do. To know that the streets of Chicago are slowly but surely getting safer under my watch makes this all worth it. To be honest with you, I was hoping to hire on another man who feels the same as I. Not only would my cases go smoother and it would be easier to catch my perps, but the clerical aspects would go by faster."

Philip tapped the counter again and Edgar refilled the glasses.

"Well, let Debra help you," Edgar suggested as he held up his glass.

Philip picked up his glass and drank. "Ah, what a bunch of palaver, I love my wife, but a woman doing detective work? Even if it's clerical, I don't think that's realistic. Think about how the city would react if the newspaper caught wind of it. I already have to grow my credibility through positive press, but if I hired my wife or even consulted with her on a case outside of secretary work, I would be the job's turkey of Chicago."

He tapped the counter again.

"You going to be able to pony up pard?" Edgar asked as he held the bottle sideways without pouring any whiskey.

"Of course I can, I closed a case two days ago and have taken care of my responsibilities."

Edgar filled the glasses and they drank.

"I understand why you wouldn't hire your wife, but it's something. At this point in your career you need some help. What ever happened to the goosecap you planned on hiring? He let you down, and now you would have to keep a pig because you have that vacant room since your son moved to Boston. By the way, how is Adam?"

Philip took off his jacket and placed it on the counter, then loosened his tie. "He's doing just fine. I'm proud of him but he's a wanton of a son. He rejects me as his father and only writes letters to his mother. After all the hard work I put into raising that boy, he leaves and crabs me on his new tailor company. As his father I should get a percentage from that company of his. And yet I pocket it. I'm more concerned about getting more cases than what that hobbadehoy is doing, which is why I tried to hire on this new fellow."

"What's his name?" Edgar asked as he lifted the bottle and raised his eyebrows, inviting Philip to another drink.

Philip tapped the counter and Edgar filled the glasses. "The lad's name is Milton. It seems that you can't find any good help nowadays. I feel as if he gulled me. Maybe you were right; I should consider my wife. No, that doesn't make sense, a woman doing detective work. Balderdash. Seems as though I am having no luck at all with my agency."

Philip wiped his face with both of his hands, picked up the glass, and drained it. Edgar filled the glasses again as soon as Philip put his back on the counter.

"The sad thing about all of this is that all I want to accomplish is justice. I want the scalawags of Chicago locked

To give a man a floorer and see him lay down the knife and fork refers to death.

up and hung for all their crimes against humanity. Let's be honest Ed, if some prick broke into your store and stole your money and food and drinks, wouldn't you want to give him a floorer and see him lay down the knife and fork?"

Edgar, with practiced knowledge of drunkenness, moved both glasses to his right and said, "With genuine sincerity pard, no, I wouldn't. All of us working folk have a monkey with a long tail, and who am I to say that any man should be confined to a specific way to feed his family? Would I be mad? Of course! Just thinking about it raises my hackles, but I wouldn't want to see that man condemned or even dead. I don't believe in the old saying, 'an eye for an eye.'"

Edgar leaned over and picked up a sign that read, "Out to Lunch," from behind the counter and walked around to the front door. He hung the sign in the window and locked the door. Philip reached down the bar and grabbed the glasses and drank both shots before Edgar returned.

"You might as well pay for the bottle if you're going to drink like that," Edgar said as he walked back behind the counter.

Philip dug his hand into his pocket and pulled out seven dollars.

"So you mean to tell me you don't believe in justice?" asked Philip.

"I'm not saying I don't believe in justice. What I'm saying is that the motivation of a criminal should determine the weight of his sentence."

"But any criminal could lie and say he had raped, murdered, or stole for his family's sake," Philip said as he took the bottle and filled the glasses.

They both drank and Philip refilled the cups.

"Let's look at the facts of the crimes that were committed. A man would not rape a woman for his family, nor would he simply murder a man in cold blood for the sake of his family. A man would kill an assailant if his family was in danger. But let's stick with thieves because, as of now, you hunt thieves. If a thief steals some whiskey, then obviously it's not to take to his wife and kids. But if that man had out-and-out stole food, water, candlesticks, wood, or any other supplies, then obviously it was to build a shelter and provide for his starving family. Should this man be convicted or hung for doing what was in the best interest of his family?"

Edgar drank the shot that Philip poured for him, then he picked up his glass, wiped it clean, and put it back under the counter.

Philip poured himself another drink and said, "I don't believe you. You honestly believe that it's fine for a man to rob the city for one family? There are so many ways to make a living in Chicago that stealing makes no sense. With all these buildings being built and elevated, a man shouldn't rob the builder of homes to build a home. He should ask the home builder for a job and take care of his family the right way."

> During this time in history, Chicago was undergoing a lift. This meant the buildings were all being raised to get them up out of the water. Major construction was everywhere.

"And what is the right way?" Edgar asked.

"His wife should work and so should he," Philip replied.

Edgar shook his head and folded his arms. "Now you're being a hypocrite Phil. You just told me that you wouldn't let your wife help you with any of your cases, yet you say a man should put his wife to work?"

Philip swallowed the drink he poured himself and said,

Women were just beginning to make their way out of the home at this time. On November 25, 1856 in New York City, Lucy Stone spoke to a crowd about the State of Kentucky's progress in women's property rights and the limited right for women to vote for school board members. Lucretia Mott spoke to women and suggested they use their new rights, stating "Believe me sisters; the time is coming for you to avail yourselves of all avenues that are open to you."

"I don't mean she should do men's work."

Edgar leaned over the counter of the bar and asked, "What constitutes woman's work?"

Philip tried to pour himself another drink but spilled on the counter. He picked up the cup and put the mouth of the bottle on the glass and poured with a concentrated expression.

"Work that don't need to be done with any muscle. Ladies stay soft and men work muscles."

Edgar reached for the bottle, but Philip grabbed his forearm and said brusquely, "Don't cheat me Ed. I bought this bottle so I'm gonna drink this whole bottle."

"Fimble-famble, you don't have to drink the entire bottle."

Philip let go of Edgar's forearm and drank his whiskey. "Humbug. No woman should be no detective. That's man work, too. Women don't do no work that takes real thought. Women can't think like us men can. They think only on pregnancy and recipes for dinners and tattle."

Edgar leaned back against the shelf behind him and folded his arms again. He looked down at his feet and asked, "What time is it?"

Philip reached for his jacket and knocked it off the counter. As he leaned over, Edgar said, "Your watch is in your vest."

Philip bellowed, "I know where my watch is, I wasn't looking for my watch!"

Philip sat up straight and reached into his vest pocket. He pulled out his pocket watch, "It's 1:22," he said. Then leaned over on the stool to pick up his jacket but was reaching for the air above his jacket.

Edgar walked around the counter and picked up the jacket.

"I don't need no damn help, get back!" Philip yelled.

"What's wrong with you now, Phil? Once a week we come together and drink and have conversations on your latest cases or just catch up with each other, but today you've got your tail down."

After putting the jacket on the counter in front of Philip, Edgar walked to the front door and took down the "out to lunch sign." With his head down and his eyes closed as though he just woke up, Philip slowly put on his jacket.

"This whole conversation's raising my hackles. There's this g'hal walking around Chicago like she's some detective. I don't know who gave her this idea, and I don't know who she thinks she is. Women stay at home to cook and clean. It's people like her who make my profession a joke. It's people like her who make it hard for real detectives like myself to get any real cases."

Edgar unlocked and opened the door. A young man stood in the doorway with his hat in his hand and a nervous look on his face.

"Excuse me sir," the young man said, "but is there a Philip Seismore here?" I was supposed to be meeting him today, but I'm so late I wouldn't be surprised if he left."

Edgar looked over his shoulder at Philip who was

pouring himself another drink.

"No, there's nobody named Philip Seismore here."

"What!?" Philip shouted as he wiped whiskey from the side of his mouth. Unsteadily, he stood up with a scowl on his face and said, "Who's there in the doorway asking for Philip Seismore, the Great Detective of Chicago?"

The young man in the doorway stepped past Edgar and reached out his hand, "My name is Milton Greene, we were supposed to meet about an hour ago but I..."

"None of that boy. The Great Seismore don't need no hobbadehoy who just learned how to fasten his sit-upons proper no way." Philip picked up the whiskey bottle and swallowed some down, then slammed the bottle on the counter. Milton looked at him with disconcertion.

"You're Philip Seismore? To think I was worried about making an impression on a rusty gut who's off his chump."

Philip picked up his hat and walked toward the door, "Dry up then, you squeaker!"

Milton put on his hat, turned around, and abruptly left the diner with an infuriated stride. Philip walked to the doorway and shouted "Chicago has no need for no more lady detectives!"

Milton stormed down the street cursing the name of Philip Seismore. "That no good old dirty scalawag. I might as well go to the station and become a copper," he fumed as he turned at the next block.

In a building Milton passed, another man with an eye on his window watched Milton waving his arms around like a dictator

WE NEVER SLEEP

speaking to a large gathering of people. From the attentive stillness of the man in the window, it was obvious he was of the same profession as Philip Seismore; however there was an intense air of experience about him.

The man opened the office window that bore the Pinkerton name and lit his cigarette with a match. He turned around to his desk, sat down, and opened a book. He picked up a pen and began to write. "What traits are required to become a good detective and in turn, what differentiates a good detective from a great detective?"

Chapter II

Modern Day

In my personal experience as a detective, I've realized it takes a special kind of person to be a detective, especially one who works undercover. The first female detective was one of these gifted people.

In the 1850s, most people had about two cows, a pig, a horse and carriage, and a good barn for hay and livestock. This is not the atmosphere or environment from which you would think a street-wise undercover detective would emerge. Growing up in a world such as this would not result in a sociologists' or psychologists' profile of a typical undercover agent for a large city National Detective Agency. A forensic psychology profiler would not have been able to associate such a person as being involved in detective work, she would seem incompatible with the job to be done.

The psychological screen-outs for undercover work are essentially the same as for police work in general. In most cases, undercover officers are chosen from nominees who are currently performing competently in their present detective assignments, and who have effective interpersonal skills. Screeners usually look for those officers who are able to work well with others as well as alone, perform with a limited amount of supervision, have a record of being truthful and reliable, and are in possession of good judgment.

Home-life is another factor. Not having conflicts at home reduces the possibility that assignments will be compromised.

Screeners especially look for street-wise candidates who can speak the language of those they are investigating. When picking the right officer for a particular assignment, screeners look for those who are age and gender appropriate and able to perform certain skills that can also come into play (Kurke and Scrivner, 1995). Training for undercover work involves focus on behavioral or psychological issues important to enhancing skill development and building personal and program resources that support the operational goals.

"It begins with personality [experts] sharing the results of entry screening and extends to looking at how personality dynamics interact under a variety of UC (undercover) scenarios. This includes effects among members of the operational team and interactive issues arising from the personal traits and styles of the subjects targeted. Training is intended to instill personal and interpersonal insights, reinforced and integrated throughout the life-cycle of the operation. Some training models employ or use a Psychological Phased Support Model in the UC classroom. Each element of the model is explained, and within each, expectations are shaped. These include establishing the legitimacy of openly involving personal issues in the operational agenda. The concept is that the patient is the operation, and all who deals with it have feelings, beliefs, and ideas that need to be communicated. The goal is to be able to know where the players are emotionally" (Kurke, 1995).

The "Early Warning Model" (Reiser and Sokol, 1971) is used to follow, monitor, and benevolently intervene as needed. "The concept of the early warning model is to recognize and correct difficulties before they become a risk to the individual's ability to effectively deal with the operation. Even the well-screened and trained personnel, due to circumstances with which they are forced to deal, may not be ready to go undercover, or if undercover, to face specific activities or to continue with their role at all. Psychological readiness indicates even the best officers can be diluted by potent, recent troubles, or less obvious circumstances that are cumulative over time" (Farkes, 1986, and Kurke and Scrivner, 1995).

As we know, undercover detectives need to be able to blend in well with the criminal element. Successful detectives have natural attributes that allow an easier infiltration of a criminal organization. Attractive women detectives are able to gain information from those who let their human sexual desires make them vulnerable. Detectives who are trained or knowledgeable of a particular criminal activity are also usually successful. For example, an attractive detective posing undercover as a female gambler would have greater success infiltrating an illegal gambling organization composed primarily of men. The detective would have her alluring looks along with the ability to speak the lingo of gamblers to work in her favor. It's human nature to like to speak with attractive people, especially those who share a common interest. Few criminals have the discipline to avoid such investigative tactics.

Chapter III

Game Changer

Writing helped Allan Pinkerton organize his thoughts when he had to make difficult decisions. This was a choice he hadn't believed he would ever have to make. It was unheard of.

The woman had weaved logic and obvious facts into a decision that felt right, though. Now that the decision was already made, he wanted to put that logic to paper. It was inevitable that people would start to ask questions and he needed well thought-out answers.

How can I call one detective good, and another of the same vocation great? What constitutes a great detective? An undercover detective would be even more difficult to classify.

One has to work well with others as well as alone, therefore, these are obviously necessary traits. But to work well in uncomfortable and dangerous situations, where one is not completely in control, is where the classification of undercover work becomes ambiguous.

A badge and a uniform gives an officer of the law a feeling of control. Citizens act correctly and carry themselves as proper individuals for fear of incarceration. However, as an undercover agent, one must walk and talk as a criminal would. One must dress and act as a criminal would. The barrier between the police and the citizen is rendered invisible or even non-existent. Also, an undercover detective should be consistently reliable. The word that encompasses an undercover detective is integrity. One should be truthful, honorable, and, without thought, display good judgment at a moment's notice. This cannot be said for every officer who wears a badge.

Pinkerton ashed his cigarette and walked to the window that was on the left side of his desk. From the same direction as the frustrated young man that he saw earlier he

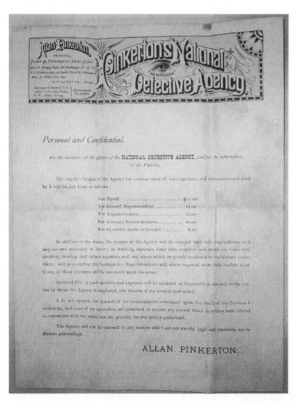

saw a drunkard. Obviously, he was inebriated because he could not walk straight and his stride was unbalanced and loose. The men and women on the street looked at him and walked around him.

The detective turned around and went back to his desk, shaking his head in disappointment at

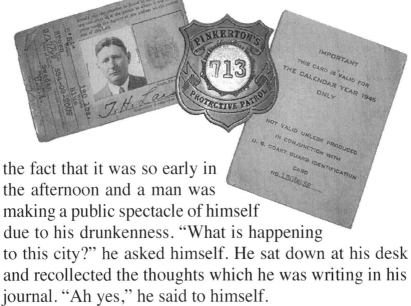

the fact that it was so early in
the afternoon and a man was
making a public spectacle of himself
due to his drunkenness. "What is happening
to this city?" he asked himself. He sat down at his desk
and recollected the thoughts which he was writing in his
journal. "Ah yes," he said to himself.

"Who am I to say that a woman cannot possess the traits
of an undercover detective? Some officers allow their
personal affairs to affect their judgment while out in the
field working a case, which in turn deters them from the
process of making just decisions. Granted, she no longer
has a family to speak of, yet as a woman, does she not
want for it in the future, and then what will happen to her
resolve? Can this woman truly denounce the aspects of
child rearing? Could this woman
dedicate her life to the work of a
detective?

And what of being street-wise
or speaking the language? She
does have a point about her age
and gender making her entry into
certain situations more feasible
than that of a man. Also, her

In 1858 the first pen-
cil with an attached
eraser was patented. Lat-
er the patent was disput-
ed saying the pencil and
the eraser had already
been invented.

Allan Pinkerton

articulation of the English language is surprising, so much so that she disarmed me. I would never have suspected I would consider hiring a woman to take on the role of a detective. But with the advancement of civilization, both economically and with an increase in individual intellect and innovation, who am I to say that a woman could not do the secretive work of investigation?

Pinkerton put out his cigarette in his ashtray and resumed his writing.

There are two types of people when it comes to detective work. There are those who have a tough constitution, and those of a more tender disposition. Those with tougher characters are far more assertive, not easily influenced by their environment, and more likely to independently persuade others do things their way. Tender-minded individuals tend to be less assertive, easily influenced by their circumstances, and welcome offerings of advice and support from their case agent.

His writing continued. I gathered from the interview with this young lady that she appeals to both types of minds. She asked the most important question in this line of work when I initially refuted the inclination of her becoming a detective. Why. This single word is what illuminates motivation of any action known to man. By her asking me why and then giving such reasoning and logic that I could not sincerely give her a rebuttal that would have been just. Extraordinary! I could not give a reply to her logic. Here was a woman with sound and irrefutable reasoning.

As he wrote at his desk, his resolve at not hiring a woman washed away. His own thoughts sorted through the facts and pointed to the one obvious conclusion. If she could handle the requirements, she would be great.

Full beards and full sideburns were very popular among men of this period. Top hats were also fashionable, such as the stove pipe style famously worn by Abraham Lincoln. Pinkerton can be seen to wear the beard, although he preferred a short hat..

Chapter IV

Kate Warne

I was born in a beautiful small town in Erin, New York, in Chemung County. In 1833 Erin was part of Tioga County. In 1875, the town had a population of about 1,556 people and was made up of rolling hills and sprawling fields. It's main business and livelihood was farming and lumbering.

Early in my marriage, my husband died in a wagon accident, leaving me on my own and in need of employment. At first, coming to terms with the death of my beloved was the most difficult obstacle I ever had to overcome. I was very distraught and knew not what to do. After a couple of weeks of reflecting and motivating myself to press onward, as I knew my husband would have wanted, I started reading through the newspapers and looking for work.

I did not have any children and was looking for a position I felt I could perform at my maximum potential. It was 1856 when I read an advertisement in the Chicago Tribune. The advertisement was placed by the Pinkerton

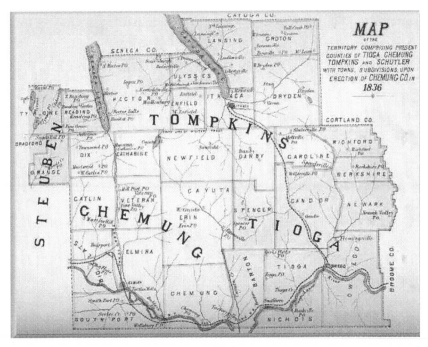

Detective Agency. My neighbors and friends believed I was looking into a secretary position, but from the beginning I intended to apply to be a detective.

Ever since I was a little girl I have wanted to be an actor. My parents, on the other hand, believed I should pursue a career that was far more practical. Even on the day I applied to the Pinkerton Detective Agency, I wanted to act. What better alternative to acting than undercover detective work? I knew I would be the best I could be in this line of work.

On the day of my interview I woke up early and chose what dress to wear. My navy blue dress was perfect. The color was in a man's tone, but the style was still elegant and tender for a woman to wear. The dress also would not sully my disposition.

It was August 23. I left my apartment early enough to go on a morning walk before my interview. I enjoyed the cool Chicago air before the sun rose and baked the city. Not many people were out and about just yet; most were still in their homes getting ready for a day of work. The breeze was fresh except on some blocks where the smell of sewage filled the air like clouds on a rainy day. I hated the city's waste issues. To look out at a body of water for inspiration is difficult when you know it is tainted with human waste. Part of me wanted to leave the city all together after the death of my husband, but some indescribable feeling in my bones made me stay.

I admired the advancement of innovation as well. To see how a group of men could raise a building was absolutely amazing. It was enjoyable to look at unfinished construction projects when no one was there working on them. It showed progress at a standstill.

I went to a park a couple of blocks away from the Pinkerton Detective Agency, sat on a bench and listened to the sound of the crickets fade and the prolonged crescendo of the birds' morning chirps.

While sitting on the bench, I started to think, Well what if I do not get the job as a detective, then what will I do? But for some reason I knew I would not be leaving that agency without being rewarded with the position. I had a talent for revolving a conversation around to my way of thinking. Allan Pinkerton would know I would do well, and if he did not, I would persuade him.

The thought of not being a detective was carried away by the sounds of the chirping birds. It was as if they were telling me not to doubt my abilities. As the sun began to rise over the horizon, I closed my eyes and waited to feel the warm embrace of the morning, the noticeable shift from the cool morning to the break of dawn. When the sun warmed my skin and made me smile I knew then that it was time to be off. My fate was in my hands, not the hands of a man, regardless of my doubts or his decisions.

After the sun had completely risen over the horizon I got up from the bench and began to make my way to Pinkerton's office. I knew there was still time before any offices opened, so my stride was slower than it was when I walked to the park. No matter how slow I strolled, I'd still have plenty of time; the agency was only a few blocks away.

On my way, I noticed there were more people out in the streets and on the sidewalks than before. It was time for Chicago's husbands and fathers to go to work to provide for their families. To think, a few months ago one of these men would have been my husband, and I would have been waiting at home. Although I miss him so much that the thought of losing him stings my eyes, I am happy to be not living the life of most of these women.

When I arrived at the agency, I saw a silhouette of a man standing in the window beneath an eye-shape that read, We Never Sleep. There was something foreboding about his presence in that window, it was almost as if he were already waiting for me to walk down this street before I even left my apartment.

I stood in the street for what seemed an eternity as I looked at him. I felt this eerie sensation creep through my body as though he knew who I was. Thoughts raced through my mind. How could he possibly know who I was among the many women walking down this street? Does he do this often, and if so he must be very intuitive. Could I persuade a man such as this to hire me, a woman, as a detective?

Just then I remembered the chirping of the birds. I reassured myself and walked across the street with a confident yet feminine stride. I pulled the newspaper clipping from my pocketbook to be sure I was at the right address, all the while feeling as if the man in the window was staring at the top of my head.

I checked the address on the side of the building. It said 80 Washington Street; I was at the right place. As I opened the door and entered the building I was overcome by the smell of tobacco smoke. I climbed stairs to the second floor and knocked on the door to my left.

"Come in," said a woman from the other side of the door.

I opened the door and walked in to find a pretty young woman sitting behind a desk. She was filling out a paper, but I could not tell what she was writing. It was obviously clerical work, which made her appear to be the secretary.

I walked up to the desk, still struggling with the smell of smoke, and asked, "Is there a Mr. Pinkerton here?"

She looked at me with beautiful blue eyes that matched my dress. "Yes he is, are you here because of the advertisement in the newspaper?" she asked.

"Yes, I was hoping to speak to him," I said. "Was he the man who was standing in the window underneath that eye?"

The woman looked back down at her paperwork and said, "Yes that's him, he usually stands there and watches the city, as if he were Chicago's guardian angel. Anyway, you can go right in dear."

The woman pointed with her pen to the door at my left and continued doing her clerical duties. There was a rush in my body that increased to the point of terror. For a few seconds I could not move, for I knew this would be a defining moment in my life. I knew that at first glance he would throw me to the female wolves of the clerical world. I also knew that if I did not present myself as

Domed skirts were increasing in popularity since their introduction in the 1840s. Hairstyles were middle parted with a bun or a braid towards the back. Cape jackets were common and covered wide skirts. The women's "bloomer" became very fashionable in 1856.

Allan Pinkerton

a woman with the intellect of a man, all would be for naught. I could feel the woman behind the desk looking at me. She must have thought I believed myself to be walking into the office of God himself. But how could I face the "man in the window"? I collected myself and walked toward the door. When I raised my hand to the door to knock, a voice arose from the other side saying, "Do come in, Miss."

I froze once again, for this was truly an amazing man. I swallowed my anxiety and opened the door.

Through the haze of tobacco I saw the man who had been standing in the window. He wore a dark jacket and dark pants with a white shirt and a dark bow tie. To my left was a leather chair; on the far side of the chair was another window, and on the floor was a dark gray carpet. The man was still staring out the window, just as he was when I initially saw him from the other side of the street. Smoke rose from his face as though he breathed hellfire and exhaled smoke. He stood on the other side of his desk next to a small cupboard. He had a beard and the most stern look on his face, almost as though he viewed the world as a disgusting, crime-ridden place.

Anxiety crept over me again, and I did not speak. I stood in the doorway petrified in fear that he knew who I was and what I had been through.

Suddenly he turned to me. It felt as though he glared

into my soul, seeing the truth of my intentions and who I really was. He knew me, and he knew why I came. He looked me directly in the eyes with the same glare that he had as he watched over Chicago. He had an oval face and a receding hairline. He walked behind his desk and put the cigarette between his lips and inhaled, then put it out in the ashtray on his desk. He raised his eyebrows, creating wrinkles in his forehead as he gave a sincere smile while raising his hand motioning to the leather chair and said, "Please Miss, sit down."

His smile was a great comfort to me because it made him seem human. He was no longer the "man in the window," but he actually had human emotions; however he was still enigmatic. And I knew if I sat down I would lose any amount of assertiveness in my dialogue. I had to be taken seriously, for what I was about to ask would be a difficult concept for a man such as this to consider.

"Sir," I said as I remained standing, "I am here for the job that was released in yesterday's newspaper."

He then sat down in the chair behind his desk and said, "It just so happens that I have a position available for a woman in recordkeeping. Are you familiar with the methods of filing?"

Now that the "man in the window" sat down, I, too, felt comfortable enough to sit down.

As I sat I told him, "No, I have not received schooling in the way of filing, nor did I come for a job such as that."

"What kind of job did you come here for?" he asked as he put his elbows on his desk and put his hands together by interlocking his fingers.

I could not help but smile when I said, "I want to be a detective." I don't know if he smiled at me because he liked my smile, the idea, or if it was just that the concept of a woman becoming a detective amused him.

While still smiling he said, "I do not hire women as detectives."

No longer smiling, I said, "May I ask why not?"

"For one," he said, "such a position is not suitable for a woman's sensitive demeanor."

I quickly stated, "With all due respect Sir, I think I'm just the person you need."

"And why is that?" he asked.

"Because I have no children and I am a widow. But more importantly, no one would suspect a woman to be a detective."

I could tell he was becoming more interested, but he played it cool as he leaned back in his chair and folded his arms.

I went on to tell him, "I have always wanted to be an actress, but my parents would never let me expose myself to what they believed was below my station. Detecting would be almost like going on stage, and the idea thrills the nature of my acting ability."

I could tell as he rubbed his beard that he was eager to hear more. He was no longer smiling and was silent. His 'guardian angel,' expression crept back over his face as he sat silently. So I continued.

"I could attend social gatherings and obtain information easily without anyone suspecting I might be working for the law. I could investigate secrets in many places to which it would be impossible for male detectives to gain access. I could also pose as a wife, a secretary, a criminal, or a member of a socially exclusive class."

Still the man said nothing. He stopped rubbing his beard and stood up. He walked back to the window where I had originally seen him when I walked into his office. He looked up at the sky, instead of at the people walking about the street.

Without looking at me he said, "I must think about this. This is completely unheard of, yet I cannot alleviate my mind of the vast potential. The unending possibilities. Go, I must think on this with thorough avidity. I shall send for you tomorrow regardless of my decision, but I must think."

Leisure fashion was becoming common upon men. A relatively new style of coat which reached to mid thigh. This coat later became the modern suit coat.

I stood up from the leather chair and walked out of his office. The secretary was at a filing cabinet behind her desk. As she looked back, I smiled and waved and so did she in response to my farewell. I walked down the stairs and out the front door. I relished the fresh air after being in a confined space of stifling smoke. I could still smell his cigarette stench all over my dress. As I thought about my request I began to doubt my skills of persuasion and just then, I heard the chirping of the birds.

The next day, after I was dressed and prepared for the events that would transpire, I heard a knock at the door. When I opened it, I was surprised to see the young lady from the detective agency.

"Good morning," she said. "Mr. Pinkerton has sent me to come and collect you. Are you ready?"

I knew then that the job would be mine, and that the course of my life had just shifted in the direction that I had planned. I went back inside, grabbed my hat, and said, "Let us be off then, shall we?"

Chapter V

Training

As he put his key into the door of the agency, Pinkerton looked over his shoulder at me. "This is *my* agency, Kate, and I will not be second guessed." He looked down at the door and turned the knob with subtle aggression.

I reached out to Pinkerton and held his arm by the elbow and said, "Did you not disagree with the notion of my becoming a detective?"

"Well primarily yes, but..."

"And did I not provide you with sound logic that even you yourself, the great private detective Allan Pinkerton, could not refute?"

Pinkerton turned halfway around to look me in the eyes and held the hand that was on his elbow and said, "Your logic is of a sound disposition, my dear, so much so that flattery will get you only so far." He let go of my hand and walked inside. I followed.

I turned around and shut the door while Pinkerton hung

his coat and hat on the rack. I immediately followed him upstairs and into his office to finish the conversation.

As I walked into his office, Pinkerton patted his vest, then his pants and checked the inside of his jacket pocket and pulled out a pack of tobacco and rolling papers. "Kate, go back downstairs and take off your overcoat and hat," he said, dropping himself into his chair.

"I may not be staying much longer depending on how this conversation goes, so my wardrobe does not matter. But it is no mere flattery that I use, Allan. With the skills you have taught me over these past two years I only use the terms I overhear while practicing my eavesdropping. Just this morning, while reading the newspaper, two men used those exact words in the park near my apartment. I overheard them on my way over this morning. This is a small example of how I apply your teachings in my day-to-day life. Do you still believe that I am not fit for this case?"

Office chairs in 1850 look very similar to those we use today.

He looked at me as I was standing in the doorway next to the brown leather chair that lined the opposite wall of his desk while he rolled his cigarette. He ran the cigarette through his lips and said, "It's not a matter of being fit for any case, it's the fact of your gender. I agreed to take you on as a detective and I even went as far as training you and taking you out to observe how I work these cases; but I did not consent to giving you major cases. At best, your position is clerical with some detective training so that you can help me with the details of some investigations."

I sat down on the leather chair, folded my arms, and

looked at Pinkerton with a fierce intensity. "I told you when we first met that I can get into locations where a man couldn't with relative ease and also that I, as a woman, am just as intuitive and observant as any man. May I ask how you would go about dealing with the Adams Express Embezzlement accusation?"

"Simple, my dear, I would attain a job and pose as an employee and work my way into the confidence of my target."

I unfolded my arms and leaned forward and smacked the back of one of my hands against the other. "Exactly," I said. "Have you ever thought about appeasing his wife?"

The smile on Pinkerton's face started to glow with intrigue, "Who, Maroney's wife? To be honest, no."

I took off my hat because I knew once I got him thinking about what I said, I had finally gotten through to him. Now I just needed to convince him to put me on the case.

He rubbed his beard, as he does when he considers my suggestions and said, "Once again the soundness of your logic is irrefutable. All right then, Kate, I will give you your first official case. Solve it as you see fit and remember all I have taught you during your training. As you know, there is an expectation of integrity to be upheld when you take on cases of my agency."

This was it. After doubting myself, after my first encounter with the "man in the window,"

after two years of training, I had finally persuaded him to give me my very own official case, I was now a detective of the Pinkerton Detective Agency.

***

The Adams Case

It did not take as long as I thought it would to solve the Adams Express Embezzlement case. Mrs. Maroney was a talkative woman who always wore extravagant jewelry and clothing. She had lovely perfumes and only ate the finest foods at elegant restaurants.

All of these observations made it easier to verify that she and her husband stole from the company, due to the extravagance of their lifestyle. I won her confidence at our first encounter in a perfume shop.

For the sake of undercover work, Pinkerton loaned me an expensive dress and bought me a fancy pocketbook. He also gave me fifty dollars in cash to show her that I was of the same caliber as her.

At the perfume shop, I picked up one of the more expensive vials of perfume right in front of Mrs. Maroney. From there, our conversation went from perfumes to restaurants and eventually she invited me to have lunch with her one day.

After about a month of meeting with her and discussing our perfumes, dresses, cosmetics, and the latest fashions from Europe, I asked her how she managed to live so glamorously when her husband did not make enough to support such a lifestyle. That is when she told me that her husband knew how to make a way when there was no way. I asked what she meant by this, and she told me everything I needed to know to arrest Mr. Maroney for embezzlement and Mrs Maroney as an accessory and conspirator to embezzlement. When I went back to Allan, he was so impressed with how I solved the case and the rate in which I closed it that he made me a full-time detective.

Case Closed

***

After a year or so, I won over many reformed criminals and women of easy virtue, gamblers, and bartenders became my informants. I solved several cases of embezzlement, murder, and grand theft. Detective work became my life.

Allan did not mind my coming into the office late because I consistently demonstrated my worth. I did not take days off, primarily because I loved what I was doing. I was acting, I was solving crimes, and I was free to come and go as I pleased.

I used several aliases, so no one knew who I really was, but many knew of my face. I could walk into dangerous locations and be greeted by dangerous men and women because I was one of them. Even though I was accepted by the underbelly of Chicago, I still maintained the tenets of the Pinkerton Detective Agency. Those principles kept me grounded.

I worked so much that my work became my personal life, and on many occasions the lines between my undercover persona and who I actually was became blurred. At first it was stressful knowing that I was undercover and not really part of the social element I was in all the time. Yet after the first few months, working undercover became second nature.

I recall one moment when I was in a gamblers' den that was notorious for housing some of Chicago's deadliest gangsters. I fancied one of the criminals, and he returned the feelings. He was a very intelligent gentleman at that.

I posed as his girlfriend for two months, and I grew to enjoy his company.

One Thursday night, we went on a walk around the city streets. No man would dare disrespect him, nor did they approach me with intimacy in mind because they knew whom I was with. This was a real man through and through.

The night was cool and breezy enough for me to wear a scarf. We held hands and enjoyed the darkness of the night that glimmered with the candlelight in the windows of houses that lined the sidewalks. I admit, I was smitten by this man even though I was undercover and was investigating him, I wanted what we had to be reality.

With my arm locked with his, and his hand in mine, I felt an intimacy that I have not felt with a man since the long-ago death of my husband. I even thought of making a reality out of what was supposed to be a case. He treated me with respect. He saw me as a real woman, not a means to an end, not a detective, and not an employee.

We walked to the park and sat on a bench. This happened to be the same bench where I sat a few years before, on the day of my interview to become a detective. I thought back for a few seconds, on the rising of the sun and the chirping of the birds. On that morning the birds' chirping made me aware of the control I had over my own destiny. The man I sat with was indeed a gangster, but I was in control of what would happen in our relationship.

I fought with the desire of my heart and the duty that was instilled in my mind. I knew if I turned my back on the agency, I would be subjected to an investigation by Allan because of whom I was with. I would be an accomplice in any crime in which my "boyfriend" would participate. But, I have been trained by an expert detective and knew how to circumvent any persecution. Would I have to tell this man what I was in order to fully be with him? I wondered.

He then looked into my eyes and said, "I don't ever want this moment to end."

I felt a fluttering in my chest that was familiar but also new. I knew he was a dangerous killer. If I were to be completely honest with myself, that aspect of him was all the more enticing. Not knowing what to say, I could not help but smile at that moment and hold him closer.

He put his hand behind my neck and kissed my lips. I didn't want this feeling to end. After about twenty minutes on the bench we stood up and began to walk on.

Just then a menacing-looking man approached us and said, "Perhaps you should take it to a room." Neither one of us was scared, for I had a pistol in my purse and he was a gangster. However, I was undercover, so I acted the part and took offense to what this other man said while adding an edge of fright, and hiding behind my escort. I turned to reached into my purse, and had just put my hand on my pistol just in case anything went awry, when I heard two gunshots.

My ears rang, and when I turned around I saw the offensive man lying dead in the grass. He had suffered two shots, one to his forehead and the other to his right cheek.

I stood in shock. This was the first time I had seen a murdered body. I had a strange feeling in my stomach. It was a flutter like before, but with a dark sickness to it. I felt as though I was going to vomit, and I almost did before my date grabbed my hand and said, "Come, Darling, we must be off. If we dally for too long, we will surely be strung up like pheasants. Don't worry about him, he has been trying to get under my skin for months."

We ran toward his apartment. The romantic infatuations I had been feeling were shattered like a large glass window. This was not the sort of man I wanted to be with. I could not help but notice the smile on his face as we ran.

From then on, he looked deformed to me. His smile was no longer enchanting, but menacing. It disturbed me to the very essence of my being. From my bones to the foundations of my emotions, he unnerved me.

When we reached the door of his apartment, he asked me if I would be okay to walk home alone because he did not want to be seen in the city streets anymore that night. I assured him I was fine to walk the rest of the way home unaccompanied. He kissed me on the forehead, gave me a hug, walked inside and closed the door behind him.

When he was gone, I felt a rush of relief. I hurried back to Pinkerton's office with urgency. On the way back, I realized that the desires of my heart were the pinnacle of foolishness.

How could I have possibly considered giving up my profession and my future to be with a demon. I knew then that I should never have confused my feelings with my work. The principles of the Pinkerton Detective Agency were there to safeguard my emotions. They were there to keep me from ruining my life. Never again would I second guess the realities of my work.

When I arrived at the agency, Allan could not help but notice something was wrong because that is just who he was, observant and intuitive. I sat down in the leather chair in his office and could not speak in my usual manner after what I saw that night.

"What happened?" he asked.

It took me a minute to understand the question; I could not stop thinking about the dead man in the park, his eyes open and lifeless, the confusion on his face. It was almost as if he were asking, "Why? Why did this happen to me."

I started to empathize with the dead man and wondered if he had a family. If so, then how would his wife and children find out about his death? I also thought about the depths of hell in which someone must find their life, to make them risk being rude to a gangster like that. How unhappy was that man?

Allan walked in front of me crouched down at my knees, and looked me in the eyes. "What did you see tonight?" he asked.

"Murder," I said. I felt as though I had been lying to Allan because I questioned myself on whether or not I would leave the agency to be with the gangster. I felt as if I was plotting to steal from Allan. Not his tobacco or money, or even the dresses and purses he provided for my undercover work, but the knowledge and skills I had learned from him over the past two years. To think I had entertained the idea of absconding with a gangster.

"Murder!? Right before your very eyes? This is exactly what we need in order to close this case. Fantastic work, Detective," he said as he went to the other side of the office and picked up his bottle of scotch.

He opened the cabinet and pulled out two glasses. "I know that witnessing a murder has left you flabbergasted and without words, but Kate," he said, as he poured out two glasses in celebration of my traumatic experience, "this is all part of what you wanted. There will be times when cases are light and relatively simple to solve. But some cases can shake you to your soul. After tonight do you understand why initially I told you that this line of work does not compliment a woman's sensitive demeanor?"

After he asked this question, my mind snapped back from the past and the hypothetical to the present reality, and I took umbrage to what he said. He approached me with one of the two glasses and handed it to me. I took it and held it in my lap. "This type of work has not and will not damage my demeanor. It is the fact that I witnessed a man die—a man who lived, who felt, who breathed, a man who was once a boy and who slept and dreamt. Any man or woman would be shaken by what I saw tonight. It is not easy to come to terms with seeing a man die. From my perspective it is far more difficult to orient myself to this when I held the hand of and kissed the murderer's lips."

Allan finished his drink and placed the empty glass on his desk behind him. He turned around and crouched down again and put his hands on both of my knees. "I understand," he said. "You are a strong woman and I will not belittle your extraordinary capacities by judging how well you perform under such harsh conditions in this line of work. Sincerely, not many men could handle what we do, and the fact that you are most proficient gives me the confidence to rely on your discretions and also your loyal integrity."

"I know that there have been times while you were on a case that you have almost compromised the pledge you made to this office," he continued. "I also know on several occasions you have thought about running away from your duty to live the life of extravagance that has been given you, and also promised to you by many of the men you are investigating. Do you know why, after you've been a detective for mere months, I have lost all my doubts of your character?" He stood up and walked to his chair. He did not sit in it but put both of his hands on the top of the chair as he stood behind it and leaned forward.

I replied, "Because I do the job right. I have informants, and I utilize all that you have taught me to close cases." After speaking, I sipped the scotch that I had been holding.

He waved his hands in the air when he said, "No, nothing so obvious, and yet it is the most obvious observation one could make. So much so that my very own secretary could, and I'm sure at this point, has noticed."

I sipped my drink again and asked, "And what is it that is so obvious?"

He walked around his desk and sat on it. He took his matches out of his pocket and picked up a half smoked cigarette from his ashtray. As he struck his match and lit his cigarette, he looked at me. He waved the match so the flame would go out and inhaled his tobacco. While exhaling the smoke he said, "You come back. You always come back." At this he sat down behind his desk, but continued. "At first I was frustrated by your tardiness. No, tardiness is an understatement. You are regularly late. Yet you come back, and not just to check in, but you come back and update me on your cases if you haven't solved them yet. You are truly an extraordinary spectacle, the likes of which I have never perceived. I am saddened that you witnessed the most egregious of crimes tonight; however, I am pleased you came back. I appreciate all you have done for me, for my agency, and for all of Chicago."

I looked down at the last swallow or two of scotch in my cup with a smile. He raised my spirits and motivated me to continue my work. He was truly a remarkable man.

Just then he said," All right, Kate, finish that scotch and let's go grab the bastard."

Chapter VI

Notable Cases

Bank Teller George Gordon

After the Civil War, one of Kate's cases involved the theft of $130,000 and the murder of George Gordon in Atkinson, Mississippi. Gordon had been struck in the back of the head with a hammer while transporting money from the bank where he worked as a teller. From the beginning, Pinkerton suspected that Alexander P. Drysdale murdered Gordon. Pinkerton did not have enough evidence to arrest Drysdale, however, so he had Kate become involved in the case.

Kate went undercover, taking the name Mrs. Potter, and struck up a relationship with Drysdale's wife. As a result of some casual conversation with the woman, Kate solved the case. She learned that Drysdale had hidden the money he had stolen from Gordon in a picture in the Drysdale home.

***

Captain Sumner Case

Captain Sumner believed that his sister, Annie Thayer, and a Mr. Pattmore were going to poison him and his wife. Sumner's sister was due a substantial inheritance if his family were to pass. Kate went undercover as a pseudo-fortune teller named Lucille, and through a series of casual introductions by Captain Sumner, she was finally able to win the trust of Ms. Thayer. She obtained enough information from her to learn that the captain's fears were substantiated. Using her fortune-teller disguise, she got Ms. Thayer to confess and name the other party involved, so Kate could make the arrest.

***

Adams Express Theft Case

Pinkerton and Kate took on a theft case in 1858 involving what was believed to be an inside job. It was suspected that an employee by the name of Nathan Delant had stolen $40,000 from the Montgomery, Alabama office of the Adams Express Company, one of the biggest transporters of goods and money. Kate went undercover and befriended Delant's wife. As a result of information Kate learned from her, the money was found 1,000 miles away from the initial crime scene and theft.

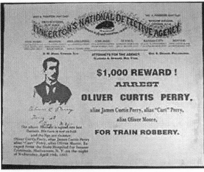

As these arrests started to pile up, Pinkerton and his agency began to obtain fame and notoriety. The Chicago Daily Democratic Press reported: "As a detective, Mr. Pinkerton has no superior, and we doubt if he has any equal in this country." Other newspapers indicated that Pinkerton "was a terror to evil doers."

***

Over the years, the Pinkerton office was involved in many cases involving missing persons. It was common for Kate to assist in spreading reward posters. Sadly, these searches were rarely successful.

Chapter VII

Running Guns for John Brown

Sixteen months after I witnessed the murder while working the case of the Chicago gambling gangster, Allan told me of his latest escapade. He was involved in helping John Brown with the escape and transportation of slaves from southern plantations to Canada. He also told me he and his wife Joan provided food and shelter for runaway slaves. I believed this to be an admirable deed. I knew that owning slaves was monstrous, but I had never had the courage to aid those who fled for their freedom. Allan told me that after he came to Chicago, his friend Robbie Fergus introduced him to abolitionism.

We were walking around the city the day he told me how and why he came to America, and also how he helped hundreds of slaves make it to freedom by providing his house as a stop on the Underground Railroad.

We went into a diner and were greeted by a large man with a bald head and a thick burly mustache. We sat at a table by the window and Allan told me about his past.

"Edgar," he said to the waiter who came to our table. "May I have two cups of coffee with some eggs and sausages. Also, a cup of water and a biscuit with gravy." He looked at me and asked, "That's all, right?" He knew it was because biscuits with gravy is what I usually ordered. I smiled and told him it was fine.

"So, Kate," he began. "I knew being an abolitionist was my next undertaking after I met a man named Frederick Douglass. He was a slave who fled to Maryland and began speaking out as a freedman on the atrocities of slavery. After speaking with Douglass for a couple of days, I agreed to aid any runaway slaves that I could."

He looked out of the window at the people walking down the street and said, "The first time I housed runaway slaves, my wife was incredibly nervous. Not because of the negroes, but she feared what the bounty hunters would do to us if we were ever found out."

"There was a storm that night. The small limbs on the trees around my house were snapping because of the wind and flying into the side of the house and windows. The howl of the wind sounded like voices surrounding our house, singing an awfully dreary and ominous harmony. The lighting spread across the sky like the hand of Lucifer, and the thunder shook the foundation of the house, as if it were the voice of God. With all of the ferocity of nature directly outside of my window, I sat and waited."

"That morning, Douglass told me that there would be runaways coming my way on their escape to Canada."

Allan took a break from his speech when Edgar delivered our breakfast. As we began to eat, he continued to tell me of his first mission as an abolitionist.

"As I sat in my bedroom, waiting for the signal from the wagon driver, I could not help but think of Scotland. At that time, leaving home was still fresh in my mind and I was still acclimating to the changes."

"Just then I saw a small flame out the window in the raging darkness. One, there's the second, and the third, I thought to myself. This was it. Here were the runaway slaves. I called for Joan and told her to prepare the table, for now was the time for us to perform our duty to these destitute people. I signaled back to the wagon and onward it came."

"When they arrived, there were four negroes and a white man. We brought them inside, gave them clean clothes, and offered them supper. While we were at the dinner table the white man told me his name was John Brown, and he thanked me and Joan for helping the men and women he brought gain their freedom. He asked if they could take shelter there for the night due to the storm, and of course I agreed."

"In the morning, we all gave handshakes and hugs. John Brown turned to me, before leaving, and told me that I had made a new friend in him."

After Allan and I finished eating we walked back to the agency. As we walked, he continued to tell me of his exploits with John Brown. I had a newfound respect for Allan and this John Brown until he informed me that Brown had killed five unarmed citizens.

John Brown

When he told me of this I was speechless. To think that the man I worked with would be in cahoots with a man who killed civilians for the sake of the abolition of slavery was repugnantly flabbergasting.

Once inside the walls of Pinkerton's office, we spoke more about John Brown. Allan sat down in his chair behind his desk and opened a drawer. I sat across from him in the leather chair, as I usually did when we spoke in his office.

He pulled out his rolling paper and tobacco and began rolling his cigarette.

"Do you believe that the end justifies the means?" I asked him after a moment. "Do you agree with John Brown that the destruction of slavery justifies any means, even cold-blooded murder?"

He finished rolling his cigarette, lit it with a match, and inhaled his tobacco. With smoke unfurling from his mouth, he replied, "It is difficult to give a concrete answer, Kate, but under extraordinary circumstances, one must take extraordinary action. If you are armed, and your attacker is not, but you shoot because you feel as though your life is being threatened, would you call that cold-blooded murder? A man does not simply kill a man for the sake of killing a man. There is and will always be motivation, which is, in a nutshell, the most important question we ask at this agency: Why? Answering this question gives us the opportunity to remove biased conclusions and assumptions and objectively discover what actually took place. In order for me to answer your question in a fashion that you will fully understand, I must ask you to again empathize with a man such as John Brown." He inhaled more of his cigarette and as he exhaled he turned and looked at the far wall of his office. "Do you agree with me, Ms. Warne?" He leaned forward with his eyebrows raised.

From his expression and body language, I could tell he

wanted me to agree with him, but I could not. Especially after witnessing the murder in the park. As I replied, "I do not know if I agree with you," Allan leaned back in his chair and inhaled his cigarette in disappointment. To appease him, I said, "However, I do not believe that you and John Brown arrived at your beliefs in an instant."

He continued to smoke as he looked at the eye on his window. He sat up, ashed his cigarette in the ashtray on his desk, and said, "Kate, I would like you to run guns to John Brown in Kansas."

"That would be dangerous," I said.

Allan went on to say, "You will be accompanied by two strong fellows. When properly made up, you could pass for an older widow, accompanied by your sons. You will be driving a covered wagon into Kansas Territory loaded with your worldly possessions and tools for farming; underneath which will be the crates of carbines."

Although I did not agree with the philosophies of John Brown, I did not want to refuse a mission. I loved what I did, and I knew that this would give me more experience and potentially additional informants to incorporate into my already wide network. I accepted and asked, "When will I begin this mission?"

Allan responded, "In a week's time."

I had had two other cases I was working on at the time. This meant I only had a week to completely close them. So I told him, "I better bring my other cases up to date."

The cases I happened to be working on were relatively simple cases. One was of a petty thief who eluded the police quite often, and the other was of a police officer who worked for some of Chicago's gangster syndicates.

***

Gangster Officer

The case of the gangster officer was a simple case to solve. I devised a plan the night that Allan told me of the gun running mission. The next morning I contacted some of my informants who were officers in Chicago's police force and asked around for any and all information they could give me on this supposed gangster officer.

My first informant was officer Mike Hooper. Mike was a man of great size compared to myself. He had small traces of silver on his sideburns and a thick, burly mustache. I assumed because of his physique that he grew up on a farm. Possibly even in a small town like the one in which I was born. He kept a homemade wooden shoe box with names, descriptions and the methods of operation of every criminal worth knowing about in Chicago. Hooper was a fountain of information.

I met him one night while I was investigating a differ-

ent case, a man who was accused of murdering his brother but had been released due to a lack of evidence. I was sitting alone in a restaurant, watching my suspect when I noticed Officer Hooper slide into the corner and begin looking around. Even though he was not in uniform, I could tell he was law enforcement. He noticed I was watching the same man, and since I had the best vantage point of the suspect, Officer Hooper asked if he could join me. We introduced ourselves and spoke about the case. He told me how the justice system had failed Chicago by letting a murderer loose on the streets to kill again, and that he, too, was gathering as much evidence as possible against the man he felt was responsible for this particular slip. We collaborated on the murder case and within a week we had gathered all that we needed to incarcerate and have it stick this time.

When I spoke to Officer Mike Hooper about the rumored gangster officer, he told me that the man's name was Milton Greene and he was a rookie. Hooper had been investigating Greene, believing him to be the reason the murderer was able to escape his first conviction. He told me Greene would take large bribes to destroy police reports and accompany gangsters to their transfer deals. There they off-loaded the products they had stolen to ensure the illegal transactions were finalized unhindered. Hooper directed me to the location of Greene's house, where I waited. I had no idea what Greene would be doing that particular evening, although my woman's intuition led me to pursue him that night.

I brought an umbrella with me so I would not be easily spotted. As there were heavy clouds that night and a strong wind, my umbrella did not make me seem conspicuous. Observing him walking out of his house in uniform, I followed him to the shipping docks where he met a group of seven men in black suits. As I kept my distance and watched, I became aware that this was a product transfer. I leaned against a tree and stared at the water while I listened intently to hear what they were saying, but I couldn't hear anything whatsoever because of the wind.

I saw the men exchange briefcases and walk away. Three

of the men in black suits walked away with Greene. They walked six blocks before they stopped at a park. Two of the three gangsters continued walking up the boulevard and disappeared, while Greene and the man with the briefcase sat and talked. The gangster opened the briefcase and passed Greene a handful of money. I could see it was a large amount of money from about sixty yards away so I knew that officer Hooper's hunches were true.

Greene got up and walked in the direction of his house. I followed him with haste as I took my irons out of my pocketbook. When he arrived at his front door he took out his house key and that was when I locked his wrists together. I told him who I worked for and what I witnessed. He slapped me with the back of his shackled hands and ran.

I ran to the police station and called out for Hooper. He rushed out from the area where they interrogated their criminals and asked me what was happening. I told him that I had bound Milton Greene in irons and he was running and that I needed his help. Without hesitation, he grabbed his helmet, placed it on his head, and we ran out of the station.

We searched for about three hours before we found him in the back of one of the gambling dens owned by the gangsters with whom he worked. He and one of the gangsters were trying to break the irons off with a hammer. The gangster dropped the hammer, put his hands in the air and slowly left the room. He knew not to openly attack an officer of the law in an establishment that dealt in stolen goods. We apprehended Greene and took him to the station and locked him up. I went back to the agency and told Allan of my accomplishment.

***

The Thief

For the case of the petty thief, I had to apply a more primal method of arrest. The petty thief's name was Timothy Atchison. His girlfriend just so happened to be an old informant of mine from when I solved the Adams Express Embezzlement case. All I had to do was entice her with a somewhat generous payment, for a woman of her social stature, and she told me where he would commit his next robbery. She informed me that he planned on breaking into the brewery. The owner lived in the apartment above the brewery, so I knew Atchison needed to get in and out quickly and most likely planned on taking whatever valuables he could carry in his pockets. After I met with the informant, I returned to the agency and shared my newly acquired information so we could apprehend our thief before he could so much as throw a rock through a window.

That night Allan and I posed as husband and wife, as we had done before, and waited on the opposite side of the street from the brewery so Atchison would be none the wiser. Allan hugged me and whispered in my ear, "He's not going to try to break in while we stand here. Let's walk up the block for a bit, just far enough to break his line of sight."

$5,000.00 REWARD FOR CAPTURE DEAD OR ALIVE OF BILL DOOLIN NOTORIOUS ROBBER OF TRAINS AND BANKS ABOUT 6 FOOT 2 INCHES TALL, LT. BROWN HAIR, DANGEROUS, ALWAYS HEAVILY ARMED. IMMEDIATELY CONTACT THE U.S. MARSHAL'S OFFICE, GUTHRIE, OKLAHOMA TER.

I nodded and we proceeded. When we could no longer see our thief, Allan ran across the street to the edge of the building so he could peer around the corner and watch to see if Atchison was making his move. He waved his arm, signaling me to go around the brewery to the other side. As I briskly walked to the other side of the building I felt exhilarated. To think I was where I was, solving cases and being able to act was such a thrill to me! I felt as though I were walking across a stage to my dressing room. I was also ecstatic at the fact that I understood Allan's signal. I knew with just a simple wave of his hand that he was planning on walking around the corner of the building, which I was now behind, to lure the thief toward me.

As I walked I could not help but smile as I reached into my pocketbook and removed my irons. I opened them so that it would be easier to wrap them around the thief's wrists as he bumped into me to try and get away. There was no guarantee that he would bump into me, but given his demeanor, I had a feeling he would. As I arrived at the other corner of the building, I remembered the chirping of the birds once again. It was a very faint memory, but I remember their calls.

When Atchison began to jimmy the lock of the brewery, Allan walked around the corner. Atchison looked at Allan and immediately recognized him, for he was the well-known "man in the window," and began to run toward me. I dropped my pocketbook and had the irons in my hand. I walked around the corner just in time to have him bump into me and we both fell. When I was on the ground with Atchison, I heard Allan shout "Kate, are you…" but before he could finish his concerned exclamation, I had already wrestled my way on top of Atchison and clasped him in irons. I never told Allan how difficult it was wrestling with Atchison that night. For an instant during our bout I was almost overwhelmed. I had to bash him in his ribs with my knee in order to maneuver from underneath him. My hat fell off during the scuffle and my hair came loose and hung in my face, over my eyes and down to my lips.

I stood up and then leaned over with my hands on my waist and looked up at Allan smiling. As he began walking toward me, he looked at me as though he had never seen me before. I tried to blow my hair from my face, but I had to use my hand to put it in a proper position. A woman must maintain an air of femininity about her. I stood up straight and rubbed both sides of my head with my palms.

I was exasperated and started looking around for my hat. Atchison was squirming on the ground shouting obscenities that I would not dare repeat, primarily because I believe it to be terribly degenerate. I then saw my hat lying on the sidewalk next to the steps leading up to the entrance of the general store adjacent to the brewery.

Allan walked to my hat and picked it up, wiping both sides of it with his hand and blowing inside to rid it of dirt. "You never cease to rise to any and every occasion and circumstance that comes your way, Kate," he said. "I say, with a connotation of absolute praise, that I never thought that I would live to see the day when a woman would wrestle a man to the ground and force irons on his wrists."

After we took our apprehended thief we went back to the agency for our usual celebratory scotch. We laughed and spoke on the events that had just transpired. After we finished our second glass of scotch, Allan told me of an idea that struck him while watching me wrestle Atchison. He didn't get into too much detail, but mentioned starting an all-female division of the Allan Pinkerton Detective Agency. After closing my cases for the week I began preparing myself for the mission to Kansas for John Brown.

***

Gun Running

On the day I was to begin gun running for John Brown, I met the two men who would be posing as my sons. When I walked into the agency, the two young men were waiting in the reception area. One of the men was standing and looking out the window, which reminded me of my first time coming into this office and seeing "the man in the window." The other young man appeared to be older, primarily because he let his facial hair grow beyond the point of mere stubble. They each walked up to me and greeted me with a smile and a handshake. The man who was standing at the window was shorter than the other, and had longer hair.

The taller man shook my hand first and said, "You must be Ms. Kate Warne. We've heard you are one of the best detectives Chicago has ever seen. My name is Bartholomew, but everyone calls me Bart."

I smiled and replied, "I would not know if I were the best detective in Chicago, nor do I have the gall to insinuate, but I really do appreciate your words. It is very nice to meet you, Bart."

The shorter young man, shook my hand with a much firmer grip. I could tell that he took me far more seriously than Bart because he only said, "Simon's the name, Ms. Warne. Nice to be working with you."

I appreciated Simon's stern demeanor. After the civil formalities, we walked into Pinkerton's office to get the details of our mission. Once we were informed of the specifics and we had received our disguises, we went out to the back of the agency and Bart and Simon loaded the carts.

First, they put the carbine crates on the wagon. Then they loaded the crates full of food, clothes, wood, gardening tools, wheat, seeds, and other supplies necessary for small farming. While they loaded the farm supplies, I climbed aboard the wagon so the boys could sit on both sides of me.

Allan stood beside the horses and said, "Remember to be as cautious as possible. Avoid any and all confrontations."

With that, we were off. We rode to Kansas without any issues or confrontations at all. We stopped at inns along the way and made it to Kansas with relative ease. Once we delivered the carbines to John Brown, we headed back to Chicago. I wanted this mission to be over and done with as soon as possible, but for some reason, on the ride back I had a severe feeling of urgency. After a couple of days of riding, we stopped at the last inn before we would reach Chicago. Simon and Bart went to the bar while I went to my room to get ready for a meeting I had arranged with an informant four days earlier. She was a reformed prostitute who worked out of a bakery in Chicago.

I went into my room and picked up the only chair and placed it by the window. I moved the table from the far wall and placed it by the chair. I lit a candle and left it burning on the table in the window to signal my informant. After about twenty minutes or so, there were three knocks on my window. It was my informant. I opened the window and said, "Hey."

She replied, "Hey, Love. Here." She put a folded piece of paper on the table by the candle and walked away. I picked up the paper and read it. "Trouble is coming," was all it said. After reading the letter, I returned the furniture to its original place and went to sleep.

Early in the morning, Bart, Simon, and I pressed onward toward Chicago. We arrived back at the agency an hour or so past midday. I told Allan that I received information that trouble was coming. His face turned hard as stone, and he dismissed me. I headed home, looking forward to my own bed. After a long mission, there is a strong sense of nostalgia when one lays in one's own bed. It seemed as though I took on the mission to return home to the comforts of my sanctuary, but alas it was but a mere bonus to my job.

The next day I arrived at the agency in the afternoon and received news of John Brown from Allan. As I sat in the leather chair and listened to what he had to say, I couldn't help but notice that he was smoking his cigarette with haste. I wondered what had happened to cause his anxiety.

"Yesterday evening when I was sitting on my couch reading," he said. "There was a sudden knock at the door. It was around nine o'clock at night, so you can imagine my surprise when I opened the door to see John Brown. He was exhausted and bleeding from his head and his torso. He also had wounds on his hands and knee. With him were eleven men, all in similar condition and just as fatigued. I let them all in for food, clothing, and to also tend to their wounds. John told me that his work in Kansas was complete and that the Kansas territory was involved in warfare. He went on to say that he was now a wanted man despised by both sides. The group 'Free Soil Jayhawkers' also resented him as a result of the problems and bloodshed he had created. After he finished his cup of coffee and his wounds were bandaged, he told me his plans to attack the federal arsenal at Harpers Ferry, Virginia, and seize its weapons to arm a slave revolt."

Allan went on to explain to me that John said he would lead the revolt along with Frederick Douglass. I knew he needed help to get John's party of fugitives safely across the border to Canada." As I digested all of this, I couldn't help but think that John Brown was a bit of a nuisance. It infuriated me to come to the understanding that when I delivered the guns, he had already wreaked havoc in Kansas and was heading for Chicago right behind me. When he showed up in need of more help, that also frustrated me to no end. When would enough be enough? I understood that his ambitions were of a noble cause, but I feared he was the type of man who would run Allan to an early grave.

I looked down at my hands as I interlocked my fingers and gritted my teeth. Allan mashed his cigarette in his ashtray and muttered, "I have to empty this; it's getting too full." He stood up and walked to the window, putting his hands together behind his back and sticking his

chest out toward the window.

Absent mindedly forgetting the full ashtray, he continued. "I need to go to the board meeting tonight. I may just find help at the Chicago Judiciary Convention."

I still could not rid myself of the feeling that all this time, money, energy, and stress would be for naught. I was so irritated that I got up from the leather chair and asked "Well, do you think you will need me for anything while you arrange all that Brown needs to escort the fugitives to Canada and execute his attack on Harpers Ferry?"

He turned around from the window, with his hands still behind his back. While looking down at his feet, he said, "No, I must think on what I must say to persuade the board leaders to help John and I. I'm afraid this will not be easy, but I do have some loyalists on the board."

I nodded and promptly left. I walked around my neighborhood for a few minutes before confining my thoughts to the inside of my apartment. Once inside, I brewed a cup of coffee, sat on my couch, and stared out the window. Before taking my first sip, I chuckled at the thought of me sitting at the window and staring out at Chicago. If anyone were to walk by and see me sitting here I wondered what thoughts would flow through his or her mind, but I bet they would be something like, "Who is that lady in the window?"

I sipped my coffee and thought about the first time I saw Allan. The "man in the window," made me freeze at the sight of him, and tremble at his insight. Then I thought about the ideology of John Brown, and I could not help but think that ever since they met, Brown had been a hindrance to Allan. Allan had not told me if Brown ever returned any favors, sent supplies, or sheltered Allan in any way. So I assumed he never did.

Another thought that vexed me was Brown killing

unarmed civilians. I could not say I condoned all the work being done for a man who caused so much bloodshed and insurrection. I understood that in both Allan's and Brown's perspective, specific circumstances justify the means, but this had become a behavioral pattern of Brown's.

The next day, I went to the agency earlier than usual. I was not working on a case but I wanted to hear what news Allan might have for me. I walked into his office and sat down. Allan seemed somewhat surprised at the hour in which I arrived. I usually come to his office after noon.

"Well, good morning, Ms. Warne," he said.

"Good morning Mr. Pinkerton," I replied with a smile. I took my hat off and put it on my lap and asked him, "So what happened at the meeting last night?"

He folded his arms, and leaned back in his chair. "All right," he said. "I explained to the leading members of the board that John was in Chicago and needed assistance to get some runaway slaves to Canada. After explaining the details of our situation, I was able to collect six hundred dollars from the members. After the meeting, I was approached by Colonel C.G. Hammond. Our agency has been effective in assisting the railroad in the past and he assured me we could have whatever we need."

To be honest, I was not happy with this news. I wished the board had rejected Allan. We should be solving criminal cases, not aiding a man who brings chaos with him everywhere he goes, but I could not tell Allan that. "That is wonderful news. So what do you need me to do?" I asked.

He unfolded his arms and said, "Nothing really, my dear, consider this a small holiday if you will."

I felt betrayed. I have been loyal, consistent, and

> The first female minister ordained in the United States was Antoinette Brown Blackwell..

> **M**ost crimes at this time were theft. There were no laws against drugs yet. Opium dens still existed.

effective, and now I was on holiday because of John Brown. Whenever Brown was around or involved or needed help of some kind, Allan dropped everything for him. I did not understand what kind of hold Brown had over Allan, and I was livid at this situation.

I nodded and began to leave the office when Allan said, "Kate." I turned around and looked him directly in the eyes. "Why does this upset you so?" he asked.

"Because I love my job," I told him. I then turned back to the door and left the office. Over the following days I walked around Chicago, I cooked and cleaned for myself as usual. The only difference was that I was aware of what I was doing. Instead of being preoccupied mentally, dwelling on a case or thinking about what my next case would be, I was present in all of my actions. I felt as though all that I have accomplished over the past couple of years amounted to nothing more than memories. I hadn't heard from Allan. Whenever I went out, I avoided the office. I felt as if I were just another woman of Chicago. I resented Allan for pushing me aside while he assisted John Brown. I resented John Brown for all of the violence he caused. I resented the entire situation.

On one of my days off, I had lunch with an informant. Not for information, but for human interaction. It was Milton Greene's old girlfriend, the one whom I paid off for information on Greene's next heist. Regardless of my feeling reluctant, I told her I was on holiday and resenting that fact. She told me that it was to be expected. She said that it was only a matter of time before Allan revealed how expendable I was to him.

I thought about what she said for the rest of the day.

Maybe I was expendable to Allan. I realized then, that I had not thought thoroughly about my future. I lived my life case by case because I did love my job, just as I told Allan when we last spoke. Maybe this was the end and that was my last time as a detective in his office.

I felt sick. I should have thought about what I would do with myself if being a detective were to come to a sudden end. I walked to the park a little before dusk. I sat on the same bench where I sat with the gangster, which was also the same bench where I sat on the day of my interview with Allan. I began to mull over what I would do next if I were not to be a detective. I had my journal with me and a pen and began writing my resignation letter.

When I finished writing, the sun was at the horizon. I closed my eyes and bathed in the last bit of sunlight the day would bring. When I opened my eyes and stood up, I saw Allan standing on the sidewalk outside the park.

Chapter VIII

The Letter

I stood up from the bench and walked toward Allan. I could not help notice the distraught look on his face.

When I approached him, he said, "Come, let us return to the agency. I have much to tell you."

I agreed, and we walked to the agency. As we walked, I thought about how Allan might view me as an expendable asset to his agency. He did not say hello, or comment on whether or not I was looking well. Nothing. His silence upset me, but something else was bothering me as well. Allan had never been one to look distraught for more than a few seconds. Maybe something was truly wrong. Was I being selfish about being sent away on holiday for a few days instead of thinking on what Allan had been through? While I was cooking and cleaning and going out to lunches and for walks, he had been working. I clenched my purse tighter. I knew then that I must listen to what happened to Allan and John Brown before I delivered my letter, a letter that had been written out of jealous spite.

We arrived at the agency. It seemed to take much longer than usual to get there from the park. I suppose it was the silence. We normally were immersed in conversation. Once inside Allan's office we both sat down. He opened his desk drawer and removed his tobacco and papers. As he began to put the tobacco in the rolling paper, he dropped his hands and let out a heavy-hearted sigh. That is when I knew something had gone awry.

"What happened on your mission to Canada?" I asked. "Was it a success?"

After I asked, he remained speechless as well as motionless. He just sat there, staring at his hands. His silence began to make my stomach flutter with anxiety. The hairs on the back of my neck stood, as though they were reaching for the wall behind my head. I felt I should give him the letter before he had a chance to fire me.

As I opened my purse, Allan looked at me and said, "John has been captured."

I closed my purse and asked, "How did this happen? Did he already attack Harpers Ferry?"

John shook his head in disappointment and replied, "Yes he did."

I began to get annoyed at the fact he was not giving me all the information of his mission. Just then he began to speak. "On the night we were to escort the runaway slaves to Canada by train, we took a wagon. We rode for a couple of hours all the way to the tracks. When we loaded the slaves onto the awaiting boxcar, John asked me if he could take the wagon."

I leaned back in the leather chair that I always sat in and waited as Allan began to roll the cigarette. "Did you give it to him?" I asked.

He licked his rolling paper and sealed the cigarette.

He ran it through his lips and lit it with a match from the box he pulled from his left vest pocket. He inhaled, then exhaled and said, "Reluctantly I did. For when he asked me if he could use the wagon, I knew he would be going directly to Harpers Ferry to meet with Frederick Douglass. I had not thought of going to Harpers Ferry myself until I realized he would be going and I could go and fight with him. I pleaded with him to let me go and take on the mission by his side."

When Allan told me that he had actually considered accompanying Brown to Harpers Ferry, I was disgusted. After years of working with him while he built the renown necessary to take on major cases, I could not believe he was willing to throw it all away for the sake of Brown. I hope my soul is not damned when I say this, but I was happy at the news that John Brown had been captured. Maybe now Allan would have his affairs in order and we could get back to work. I had missed working cases and going undercover, especially with Allan.

He then continued. "John refused to let me accompany him to Harpers Ferry, he put his hand on my shoulder and told me that was not the assignment." Allan stopped and leaned back in his chair rubbing his eyes. "I was distraught at this fact, and John said to me, 'Tell all you trust to lay in their tobacco, cotton, and sugar, because I intend to raise the prices.' I smiled at what he said and he did the same. After he let go of my hand he climbed

Senator Charles Summery spoke out against slavery. Abraham Lincoln gave a speech in which he spoke of his dislike of slavery and where slavery got it roots from.

Elizabeth Cady Stanton continued her beliefs that slavery should be abolished. She also was a pioneer promoting women rights.

The year 1856 was an important year. The United States elected its 15th President of the United States, James Buchanan, and Russia signed the Peace of Paris, ending the Crimean war.

onto the wagon and whipped the team of horses and raced away. I knew that would be the last time I saw him."

As he inhaled his cigarette and put it out in his ashtray, it was obvious to me that Allan took John's capture hard, but I could not help but feel as though it was for the best. Allan went on to say, "Yesterday I received word that Frederick Douglass did not arrive to help John at Harpers Ferry and that John had been captured and is facing execution by the noose. We must do what we can in order to save him from a fate such as this. A good man is about to die because he fought for liberty and justice. I cannot sit idly by while a dear friend of mine dies for his beliefs. This is an injustice."

I was stunned. I had thought our conversation would conclude with Allan resuscitating his priorities and affairs and things would return to normal. But this, I couldn't believe! He planned to rescue John Brown from execution, after he was rightly prosecuted and convicted? It was too much for me to bear. Allan had lost sense of our aspirations and ambitions for the city of Chicago, the state of Illinois, and the nation itself. I knew then that I would most definitely resign that day.

Allan stood and paced the office as he said, "I have already spoken with the other detectives, they have somewhat agreed and detective Webster is by my side through and through. I wanted to ask you directly if you would aid me in this endeavor. I could really use your ability to move in and out of crowds undetected for this mission. What say you Kate?"

I didn't know his plan nor did I honestly think he had a plan. I then thought about Allan's perception of my expendability. I was just another tool in his shed, an axe to chop down trees, or a hammer to drive a nail into a post. I was a mere object to Allan and this mission was proof of that.

So I asked him, "What do you think your chances of success are?"

He stopped pacing the office and looked at me as he stood behind his desk and said, "I do not conceive plans that are doomed to failure!"

I replied, "What are your chances of freeing John Brown and escaping alive?"

He said nothing, so I continued, "This mission is not about freeing John Brown. It's about your wish to die for a cause. If that's what you are determined to do, go ahead. But you cannot take five others to their deaths with you!"

He turned his gaze away from me and walked to the window. He said "I understand your reluctance to participate and it would not be held against you if you decline. There would be no repercussions in regard to your employment."

The entire conversation frustrated me to no end, but Allan's inability to see what was obvious and standing right before his eyes made me lose my temper.

I shouted, "Because there will be no agency! You and every man you take with you will be dead!"

Allan turned from the window, red in his face with anger, and said, "That is it! I've tried to be understanding of your animosity toward John but I will not tolerate a woman shouting at me as though I am a child in my own office! You're fired!"

I reached into my purse to remove the resignation letter, but something stopped me. I glared at him and then left the office absolutely livid. I slammed the door behind me as I stormed through reception, down the stairs, and out of the building. I walked to my apartment and began to clean with a rage I had never felt before.

The audacity of that man to not only treat me like an expendable tool in his backyard shed, but to ask me to take on a suicidal mission. Allan Pinkerton had compromised himself for the sake of a man who deserved to die, and I refused to be around such lunacy.

A few days later, Allan came to my apartment and asked if we could talk. I invited him in and poured him a cup of coffee. We sat on my couch and I gave him time to collect his thoughts. As he swallowed the coffee he nodded his head as though he were thinking, Good coffee. I poured my cup and I added a scoop of sugar and sipped mine as well. We sat for a few moments in complete silence. I was not going to be the one to speak first. Eventually, he placed his cup on the table in front of the couch, and I did as well. Finally, exasperated, he said, "I did not attempt to follow through with a jail breaking plan to free John Brown. He will be hung on December 2nd."

After he said that he picked up his cup of coffee again and sipped it. I could tell by the way he spoke that he had come to terms with all that had happened. Not only with Brown's impending execution, but with his and Brown's entire relationship. I felt as though Allan realized this was going to be Brown's fate if he continued to carry on the way he had. There was a sense of restoration in my apartment that morning as we drank our coffee and spoke.

"Will you come back Kate?" he asked. "Not only do I need you there, but I can't imagine the place without you." He put his cup of coffee on the table and put his hand on my thigh, saying, "Come back, Kate."

He looked at me with an expression I had not seen

before. It was a gentile and fragile look of longing. He looked like he had lost everything and was working on redeeming himself. I felt a flutter in my chest. Even though his eyes were softer than usual, they were still as piercing as they were the first day I met him. I studied his prominent nose and strong jaw, then looked down at his hand on my thigh. He'd never touched me like that before. Sure, he'd put his arm around my shoulder while we worked under-cover, but this was far more intimate. I bit my bottom lip and said, "Yes."

Allan began to rub my thigh as he looked down at my legs and then back into my eyes. He leaned in closer to me and I to him. I put my hand on top of his hand and our lips met. It was as though time stood still and there was nothing outside of our kiss; no Chicago, no reality. That moment in time seemed to last for an eternity. Just as I began to drift in the fantasy that was born from the kiss, we separated and looked into each other's eyes.

My neck, face, chest, and shoulders were on fire. I knew I had begun to blush and he smiled at me. I had never seen this side of Allan before, neither of us knew what was to happen next because I was a widow, and he was married. However, none of that mattered at that point in time because I was going back to the agency regardless of what would transpire.

Chapter IX

Rose Greenhow and Little Rose

Born in 1814 in Montgomery County, Maryland, Rose Greenhow was a spy for the Confederate army. Like Kate Warne, she was able to use her attributes and abilities to cultivate friendships and mingle with generals, senators, and other individuals that had pertinent information regarding troop movements and union activities. Completely undetected, she passed on military secrets to her contacts within the confederacy.

Like many undercover operatives today, she had a handler. His name was Thomas Jordan. In 1861, Jordan gave Greenhow complete control of a pro-South spy ring in Washington, D.C. Many accounts indicate that through her her spying accomplishments, Greenhow was able to provide enough information to the confederates that she is credited with the victory in the First Battle of Bull Run in July 1861.

Allan Pinkerton was on assignment in Washington and

was asked to follow her on one occasion and observed a Union officer handing her some papers. He knew that Greenhow was a traitor and was providing documents that indicated where Union army strongholds were around Washington, D.C. When the Union officer parted from Greenhow, Pinkerton followed him. The officer noticed Pinkerton following him, however, and began to run. Pinkerton chased him to the provost-marshal's station.

As it turns out, the officer Pinkerton was pursuing was the Captain of the Guard. When Union soldiers observed Pinkerton tracking their captain, they quickly surrounded him and the other detectives, and placed them under arrest. From jail, Pinkerton was able to get a note to Thomas Scott in the War Department, who knew Pinkerton from a case they had worked on together. Scott then arranged their release.

After he was set free, Pinkerton continued his pursuit of Greenhow. He followed and confronted her as she was walking home one day. He asked if she was Mrs. Greenhow. She replied yes, and asked him who he was, at which point Pinkerton informed her she was under arrest. He brought her the rest of the way to her house and told her to open the door, which she did. A thorough search of her home on August 23, 1861 produced coded messages and a leather diary that contained accounts of Union troop movements and military operations. Seven pages of War Department documents indicating plans to increase the size of the Union army were also found as well as many letters tying her to spying activities.

These findings led to the eventual questioning of the Captain of the Guard by Thomas Scott, who caught him in various lies. The captain was ordered to surrender his sword and was placed under arrest. The confiscated documents also led to the questioning of many other influential individuals who were sharing military secrets with Greenhow. These included Senator Henry Wilson of Massachusetts, whose confidence was gained by Greenhow through romantic advances; a dentist named Aaron Van Camp; government clerks William Walker and F. Rennehan; George Donnellan; and banker William Smithson. All were subsequently charged, and those who were women were kept under house arrest in Greenhow's home. Greenhow was eventually transferred to the Old Capital Prison, a small brick building directly across the street from the Capitol. A sad note about this case, Greenhow's daughter Little Rose was incarcerated with her mother in the prison. It was feared that if Greenhow was tried for treason, she

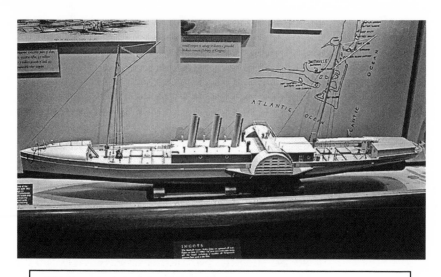

This is a model of the British blockade runner "Condor" that ran aground near Fort Fisher in 1862. She was attempting to bring supplies to the Confederates in Wilmington, NC.

would divulge her numerous secrets to her only living heir. Many of these secretes involved high-ranking union officials. After her eventual release, Greenhow was returned to Richmond and reunited with Confederate leaders. She was given much praise, especially from Jefferson Davis, who saw that she was rewarded for what he called her "valuable and patriotic services, with twenty-five hundred dollars from the Confederate secret funds.

Greenhow's spying career was far from over, however. She was later sent on a secret mission to Europe. It is reported she met with Napoleon III and Queen Victoria while in London. As was customary for Greenhow, she attended parties and was invited to discuss politics. It was also reported that she met with Lord Granville of the House of Lords, with whom she became romantically involved.

Greenhow later wrote letters to Jefferson Davis indicating that both England and France had turned against the

South. During her time abroad she was very concerned about Little Rose and thus placed her in the Convent of the Sacred Heart in Paris. It was a Catholic boarding school that housed approximately two hundred students from across Europe. After remaining in Europe for two years she boarded the Condor, a boat noted as a blockade runner, on August 10, 1864.

The boat was a three-funneled steamer, newly built and on her first trip as a blockade-runner with Captain Augustus Charles Hobart-Hampden, known only as Captain Roberts. While the ship was traveling toward Washington, it battled heavy seas in Cape Fear, the entryway to Washington. During the storm Captain Roberts saw another ship that he believed was a Union gunboat. He took an evasive action, which caused the Condor to go upon a shallow inlet bar. However, what he had thought was a Union gunboat was actually the wreck of the blockade runner Nighthawk. What he should have been worried

about was the USS Niphon, an actual Union gunboat whose crew observed the Condor in trouble and began to close in on her. On shore, Confederate troops saw what was about to take place and started firing upon the Niphon.

During the altercation, Greenhow and two other confederate spies who were accompanying her asked the Captain to lower a lifeboat for them to use to escape. The Captain did not want to comply, but at Greenhow's

Where Rose washed ashore, as it looks today.

persistent pleas, he finally did as she wished. She and her two comrades entered the boat, but ran into trouble before they could reach land. The lifeboat eventually sank within sight of shore.

Although Greenhow was reported to have been a good swimmer, it was said that she had two-thousand dollars in gold sovereign fastened to her waist which weighed her down. She drowned while attempting to reach shore. The other two spies were able to reach shore safely.

When her body washed ashore, it was discovered by a confederate soldier who removed the gold and pushed her back out into the water. When the Confederate soldier learned about this woman being a hero to the Confederacy, he confessed and returned the gold to his supervisors.

Greenhow's body eventually washed back on shore. When searchers found her body once again, they discovered a copy of her book, My Imprisonment, which held a note to her daughter Little Rose that read:

"London, November 1st. 1863: You have shared the hardships and indignity of my prison life, my darling; and suffered all that evil which a vulgar despotism could inflict. Let the memory of that period never pass from your mind; else you may be inclined to forget how merciful Providence has been in seizing us from such people."

Rose was laid to rest with military honors on October 1, 1964, in Oakdale Cemetery in Wilmington, North Carolina. It is reported that a Confederate flag was draped over the coffin, and every Memorial Day since her burial a wreath of laurel leaves has been placed upon her grave for her work as a spy for the Confederate army.

As would be expected, many back in Washington who had been involved with Greenhow were relieved to hear of her death. The upper echelon of Washington officials now knew she could no longer defame them and their office.

Rose Greenhow was in good company. Other confederate spies have since surfaced, such as Sarah Antoinette Slater; Olivia Floyd, who lived to be eighty-one in the year 1905; Ginnie and Lottie Moon; Nancy Hart; Antonia Ford and Laura Ratcliffe; Belle Boyd; Clara Judd; and Loreta Velazquez.

Chapter X

Team of Five

It was the month of January, the year 1861. John Brown had been hanged two years earlier, on December 2, 1859, and his corpse had hanged publicly for two months before being cut down on February 27, 1860. It had been about a year and a half since Allan came to my house and asked me to return to the agency, and all of our affairs had returned to normal. He and I had been working case after case. We were making good money, and going undercover together more frequently. We posed as husband and wife on cases that did not require it, but I didn't mind working intimately with him. I assumed it was easier for us to be together romantically while undercover than outside of work. I thought nothing of it because I knew that we could never be together in the "real" world, and I felt as though Allan knew that as well.

One morning I walked into reception and saw that the wastebasket was filled with telegrams from a man named

No picture has been possitively identified as Kate Warne. It is possible that this photo may show her. Pinkerton sits in the chair on the right, and the woman behind him is believed to be Kate.

Samuel Felton. I was curious, so I read one, then another. They were all asking the same question; every last telegram. Samuel Felton was repeatedly requesting to know what Allan's plans were to protect his railroad.

I walked into Allan's office, holding the telegrams, and asked him, "Why can the agency protect the entire Illinois Central Railroad and not Mr. Felton's line, which is less than a quarter of the length?"

Allan was leaning back in his chair with his feet on his desk, smoking a cigarette, wearing his "guardian angel" expression. After I asked him the question, he took his feet off the desk and leaned forward in his chair. He put his elbows on the desk and placed his left hand, which was holding the cigarette, on his right forearm and hunched over his arms. He inhaled his cigarette and said, "Because it would take too many men to protect such a rail line due to the many bridges and multiple points of vulnerability along Felton's line." As he spoke, the smoke from his cigarette unfurled from his lips.

In the telegrams I had picked out of the wastebasket, there was no information as to why Mr. Felton wanted to contract with the agency for the sake of his railway. I had deduced that Mr. Felton had some enemies who wanted to see him bankrupt, since he was a successful man. But that deduction was nothing more than fantastical speculation.

I could tell Allan was reluctant to accept this contract, so I wanted the facts. "Why does this Samuel Felton want to contract with us?" I asked.

"Felton believes that some Maryland secessionists are plotting to destroy remote sections of his railway," Allan explained. "Also, Abraham Lincoln is supposed to travel on his railroad in less than a month to be inaugurated as the sixteenth president of the United States. The train would depart from Chicago and arrive in Washington, and Felton wants to make sure the train is secure."

I recommended taking the contract despite the difficulties, just for the pay and renown. I also suggested he let Mr. Felton know that the offered payment was not enough for such a difficult assignment, and that Felton would be indebted to Allan.

Allan seemed to think about it. He put his cigarette in his ashtray, leaned back in his chair, and said, "All right then, I'll send Felton a telegram and arrange for five people to work undercover as Southerners returning to Baltimore. I will be sure to tell him that we shall follow my agency's procedures."

So I sat in his office while he composed a telegram explaining to Felton how he intended to protect his railway. As Allan worked on the telegram, I couldn't help but think of how over the past year, Allan had been hiring more women to be detectives at the agency. I was to be a mentor to the ladies due to my experience and my success at closing cases. To me it was a personal revolution. I was amazed by the fact that I came from a small town, became a widow, doubted my ability to become a detective, yet would be instructing other women on how to work undercover.

Allan finished the telegram and we sat and waited for a response. When it arrived, it said we should meet with him the next day and discuss specifics in person with this, as Felton called it, "so-called team of five."

So Allan dismissed me and I went to work for the rest of the day. I talked to many of my informants around Chicago in order to develop leads for some miscellaneous cases. The next morning I entered Allan's office rather earlier than my usual midday appearances to find Mr. Felton sitting in my leather chair by the door in front of Allan's desk. I must admit, when I saw a rather plump man with a cat's tail of a mustache sitting in my chair I was a bit annoyed. However, after thinking for a second I smiled because I realized it was just a chair.

Allan and Mr. Felton stood as I closed the door behind me. "Sam," Allan said. "This is Ms. Kate Warne. She was the first female detective I have ever hired. She has not once let me down, nor betrayed me. She has revolutionized many aspects of undercover work, and how we, as men, should view women."

I began to blush at Allan's words. Mr. Felton leaned over and took my right hand and lifted it to his lips. As he kissed the back of my hand, he looked me in the eye and said, "The pleasure is, of course, all mine, Ms. Warne. A woman of your disposition must have fascinating techniques of motivation to sway Allan into hiring you. But alas my dear, I don't think a mission such as this would be proper for a lady."

I snatched my hand away but said nothing. For the sake of this contract and out of respect for Allan, I held my tongue. Felton's charming smile became the grin of a pig in a pen receiving its early morning slop. Just then, outside Allan's office, I heard the reception door open and the sound of four or five other people walking across the wooden floor. As the sounds of the footstep's came closer to the office door, I realized they were my fellow cohorts of the agency. One of them knocked on the door and I walked around Allan's desk and stood by the window that displayed his trademark eye, the very same window that he always stared out, as the "man in the window." After I took my position at the side of Allan's desk, Mr. Felton opened the door and in came Hattie Lawton.

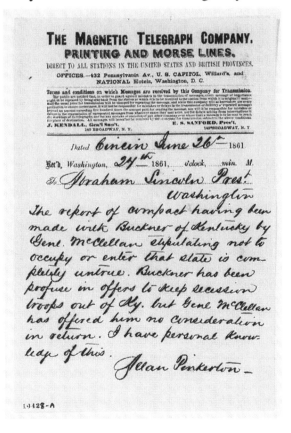

A letter from Pinkerton to Abraham Lincoln

She was one of the other female

detectives that Allan employed. After I helped close the case of the petty thief, Atchison, Allan mentioned hiring more women to be detectives. She was the second to be hired after me. Following Hattie was Pryce Lewis. Lewis was a cousin of Bart, the young man who accompanied me on the gun running mission to Kansas. I'd seen him a few times in the office and on the streets working cases and we had become acquaintances, but this would be my first time working with him on a case. After Pryce entered the office, John Scully followed. Scully was a very humorous man. When working undercover, he would choose the most peculiar and comical of disguises. He even dressed up as a woman once just so he could empathize with women. Not only was he strange and funny, but he was also incredibly witty. The level at which he could deduce an inquiry could lead someone of a more simplistic intelligence to believe that he was clairvoyant.

As everyone entered the office and got settled, I saw a man sitting in reception who must have come in with everyone else. But before I could distinguish who it was, Mr. Felton closed the door. I turned my attention back to my coworkers as they introduced themselves to Felton.

Scully said to Allan "Do you have any scotch in these cabinets, Al? You Scots and your scotch, ha! Oblige me in a drink will you? You always have the good stuff, too."

"Get out of my cabinets," Allan snapped. Scully would always embarrass Allan when he could, usually in front of clients. Mr. Felton looked at all of us with disdain.

He said, "You cannot possibly expect me to consider this, Pinkerton! Women?! Ms. Warne is lovely, as is Ms. Lawton, but are women going to protect my rail line from these fire-eating secessionists? Pinkerton, we are one week closer to civil war than the last time we met, and you bring me a force of five?"

Again, I looked at Felton as though he were nothing more than a pig in pants with a mustache. Allan sat down in his chair, and Felton sat down in my chair, while Hattie, Pryce, Scully, and I stood.

Allan then said, "You telegrammed me asking what my plan was for protecting your railroad, and I told you that we will be in disguise as Southerners returning from Baltimore. I have assembled a healthy diversity here, so much so that you yourself believe that you should not consider following through with this plan. That is all the proof you need in my agents' abilities as detectives; because everyone that you see here is an accomplished undercover agent."

The 1st female medical school was opened in 1850.

The 1st locomotive runs from the Atlantic Ocean to the Pacific Ocean on the Panama Railway in 1852.

And in 1858, the first use of fingerprints as a means of identification is made by Sir William James Herschel of the Indian Civil Service in India.

Mr. Felton sat quietly and listened to what Allan had to say. "My detectives and I," he continued, "will mingle with the Southerners and learn of plans they may know about. Once we arrive in Baltimore, we will also speak to those who most likely have knowledge of, or some connection with, persons and secessionist plans. Once this intelligence is gathered I will let you know."

I looked down at Allan as he sat in his chair and reached for a half-smoked cigarette in his ashtray. He struck a match, lit the cigarette, and inhaled his tobacco.

As he exhaled, Mr. Felton said "All right, Pinkerton. I still believe that this plan is unorthodox, but I'll trust your judgment."

Allan inhaled the tobacco from his cigarette again, and as he exhaled the smoke he said, "You have no choice."

Mr. Felton turned his head from Allan and sucked his teeth, because everyone in the office knew that Allan was absolutely right. Mr. Felton was not in the position to demand or negotiate. He needed a plan, and Allan had one.

"So what's all this gonna cost me, Pinkerton?" Felton asked.

Allan shouted, "Bangs!"

I then realized who the man sitting in reception was. He was Mr. Bangs and his job was to write up contracts for Allan and his clients. He opened the door and walked into the office.

"Sam, this is Mr. Bangs," Allan explained. "He will draw up the contract necessary in order for us to proceed with our agreement."

Mr. Felton nodded and said, "All right. Now that we have come to terms with what will be done for the sake of my railroad, I will come back tomorrow and review the contract to conclude

Harriet Tubman arrived in Auburn NY, on her last mission to free slaves on the Underground Railroad, and evaded capture for 8 years.

President Lincoln declared slavery in Confederate states unlawful.

Behind the scenes, Pinkerton and Kate had many connections to President Lincoln and assisting slaves to freedom.

our negotiations and get things underway."

Mr. Felton removed his pocket watch from his vest and walked out of the office. Allan dismissed all of us after Felton left. I was the last to leave and overheard Allan telling Mr. Bangs to write up a contract, instructing him to make the rate considerably higher than usual. I waited outside in reception for Mr. Bangs.

After about ten minutes, he walked out of Allan's office. We strode out of the building together and I asked him to include a clothing allowance. He agreed without objection because he knew I had a cunning intuition. After he agreed, he walked away and I looked up at the window of the agency and stared into the retina of the trademark eye. For some reason, this mission, with a team of more than three, excited me. As the wind blew, I listened for the chirping of the birds.

Chapter XI

To Baltimore!

On January 30, 1861, early in the morning, Pryce and I arrived at the Chicago train station, headed to Baltimore in the disguise of Southerners. I was posing as a southern belle and took on the alias Amanda Baker. Pryce was an English baronet and for the sake of preserving our mission and each other's ruse we did not know one another's aliases.

The sun had just risen over the horizon when we arrived at the station. Chicago carried an orange hue on all of the buildings, windows, trains, dirt, animals, wagons, grass, and stones. It gave me a sense of nostalgia to reflect on the day of my interview on mornings like this. But during the mission I have no time for idle thoughts. We waited in line behind a few southerners. Pryce and I, could not help but try to eavesdrop on their conversations in an effort to be sure that they themselves were not secessionists.

There was a man who wore glasses standing directly in

front of me with large lambchop sideburns that protruded past his ears. He also wore glasses and had a thick mustache. He wore a brown suit with black loafers and his hair was long and slicked back and downward, and the ends of his hair curled at the nape of his neck. The man standing next to him was as tall as Pryce and he wore a dark blue suit and a hat. His hair was black and his face was cleanly shaved. I leaned forward a little as I raised my fan and covered my face below my eyes and listened.

The man in brown said in a southern accent, "I can't take much more of this heat. Once we get on that train there, we gon' be just fine riding in the wind with them windows down. But like I was sayin', Charlie, I made a decent little something to take back to Baltimore for the Mrs. They got some good gambling halls 'round Chicago."

There was nothing more I needed to hear, these men were here to escape the confines of their responsibilities to their wives and children. Pryce then looked at me and pursed his lips, shaking his head, indicating that the two men were not secessionists, nor were they affiliated.

Southern style dress in 1850s

I leaned to the side so I could look at the railcar entry steps where people entered the car one by one. It was quite warm outside, as the man in brown said, and I fanned myself in order to stay cool. Pryce's brow had already begun to excrete beads of sweat as though he had just been walking in a light rain. The dress that I was wearing was of the latest Southern fashion. It was rather low cut so it kept me cooler than a full dress would, but the fan wasn't helping much, it seemed to only wave more hot air in my face.

I glanced around wondering where the others were. I looked up at Pryce and asked, "Where is everyone?"

Pryce leaned over to me and said, "Hattie, Scully, and Allan plan on taking the early afternoon train. Allan never explained why we split up and took different trains, but he knows all of our abilities better than we know each other's, so I figured he had a valid reason."

We slowly approached the railcar entrance and before we got onboard, Pryce whispered to me, "Let's sit in different seats away from each other. No point in listening in on the same conversations."

Nodding, I turned my head to look at the smoke trailing in the wind from the engine of the train like a ribbon. When we boarded, there were several southerners and some native Chicago civilians. It was difficult to find a seat. For some reason, I never really liked trains. This train was oak brown on the inside and the windowsills were forest green. The carpet matched the windowsills, and all of the booths faced each other so that those who sat in front of someone could have a face-to-face conversation. The thing that irked me the most was the fact that almost every booth had at least two people sitting on one side and two on the other. While, this would make information gathering for my mission that much easier, personally it was too cramped and I, like most people, enjoy some space to move my elbows.

I choose one of the only seats that was completely vacant and closer to the engine room. It faced the only exit and entrance of the train car. There was a man and his wife in the seat in front of me. As I sat down, I smiled and said, "How y'all doin' today?"

The man tipped his hat and replied with a smile, "Just fine, Ma'am."

His wife held a pair of white gloves in her hands and said, "Hi," with a smile.

Pryce also chose one of the few vacant seats and it was directly in the middle of the car. We both sat by the window in our respective seats. A couple minutes went by as we waited for the train to depart. Then a woman, two men who wore very clean suits and top hats with pins on their lapels, and a mother and her daughter boarded the train.

The woman, who was the first of the group to enter, sat next to me. She had brown hair and green eyes. She wore a white bonnet and a light blue dress. Her shoes were fashionable, yet practical. I give all the thanks of my fashion sense to Mrs. Maroney a few years ago, because really, that's all we talked about until she told me how her husband was embezzling from the Adams Express Company.

The two men in the elegant suits who wore the same pins sat in two different seats. Why are they wearing the same pins, and what exactly are on those pins, I wondered. Because of the distance in which I sat from them, I could not determine what the pins were.

They sat in seats far from me and directly in front of Pryce. I looked over at Pryce as the mother sat next to him and lifted her daughter to her lap. Pryce was looking around the train, but his back was to me so he never looked at me. I could tell that the same two men who caught my attention had caught his as well. I knew that his looking around was to avoid inconspicuous staring at the two elegant men.

Next, a man in glasses appeared on the train. He wore a straw hat and a bowtie, a white collared gingham button down shirt, and gray pants and jacket. He held a newspaper underneath his arm and a case in his hand.

I looked over at Pryce and he looked at the man who just boarded the train as I did. There was something peculiar about this man. I could not help but stare at him. After a few seconds I turned away and looked out the window of the train with a smile.

The funny-looking man sat in a seat next to an elderly gentleman who was sitting in front of one of the elegant men. There was so much clamor in the railcar that I really could not make out what most of the people sitting farther away from me were saying. It was an incongruous symphony of conversation and laughter.

After everyone boarded, the train finally left the station with the shriek from the train whistle, and we were off to Baltimore. I thought about how difficult it would be to gather information among so much noise. Everyone was conversing but how could I possibly eavesdrop when several people opened their windows, which I must say was a refreshing way to cool down. I figured the best way to collect as much knowledge as possible about the secessionists' plot would be to speak to those around me, so I greeted the lady next to me with the usual pleasantries. The husband and wife who sat in front of us were wrapped up in their own discussion, so I didn't have to incorporate them in what I wanted to discuss, but at the same time it would be beneficial to listen to those whom I could clearly hear.

As I spoke with the woman by my side, I came to discover that her name was Mrs. Josephine Hill, and I told her my name was Amanda Baker. The ride from Chicago to Baltimore would take a day and a half, so I knew I would not have to rush into my attempts at extracting information from my new friend. However, I did wonder who her husband was. That was going to be my next question, but before I dug deeper, I spoke about the weather.

"It sure was scorchin' outside this mornin'," I said. "I felt like I was about ta wilt, even in the shade! And my fan here is worth 'bout nothin' since all it did was wave more hot air in my face."

Josephine giggled and replied, "I know exactly what you mean. At least you ain't in a full dress like me. I wish I would've went out for a mornin' walk before I just put on any ol' thing."

I asked, "You go on mornin' walks often?"

She nodded yes as she pulled her fan out of her purse and attempted to cool herself. I noticed that she crossed her legs as she fanned her face and began to kick her left leg, which was on top of the right. I wondered why she was doing that. I noticed that all she had was a purse, just as I had, which was when I realized that she was waiting for the Pullman porters to come and serve us.

I had never cared for the services of the porters, primarily because they were all African Americans. My feelings were not motivated by the color of their skin or of the profession itself, but were more directed at those of us who sat in our booths and were served by men who appeared to be capable of so much more than attending to the fat, greedy, and irresponsible people on these damned trains. I understand that this profession is a way for them to provide for their family, but they are men just like the man who was sitting in front of me with his wife.

At this point in our voyage, it was about high noon. I could tell because the sky was solid blue and the clouds floated in the sky like billowy splotches of cotton. After about twenty minutes of Josephine and I making small talk, the Pullman porters came from the train car behind us, offering drinks and food. Josephine ordered a chicken sandwich with tea, and I asked for the same thing except I wanted water. I didn't pay any attention to what the couple in front of us ordered because I was more focused on Josephine's response to my ordering the same meal as her. She looked at me with a smile and a nod to signify our correlating affinity with a chicken sandwich.

I said to her, "It's so much easier to eat a sandwich on a train than a meal with a knife and a fork, don't you think?"

She responded, "Of course, I always order a sandwich on a train and on top of that the bread will stick to your ribs after you finish your drink."

As we waited for our food, we continued to talk about things that had absolutely no merit, but I knew that my plan to gather information was working because she was becoming more friendly as we neared Baltimore.

After we ate I decided to take a fake nap. I wanted to think about how I would ask her about her husband and for information on secessionist plots to destroy the railroad. Josephine began to knit a scarf or maybe a sweater, I could not tell what it was because it was just a small piece of a mysterious project at that point.

What began as a fake nap became a real siesta. When I awoke it was nighttime. I hadn't realized how tired I was until I slept.

Josephine said to me, "Hey there! You sure were tired."

I had been leaning on the windowsill, so I sat upright and looked at the couple in front of us and they were asleep. I replied to Josephine, "I sure was. The funny thing is that I didn't even know I was that tired."

She smiled and said, "That's when you sleep the best, don't ya think?"

I nodded and then began to inspect the train and its passengers. The two elegant men were awake, as well as Pryce and that funny-looking man. As a matter of fact, the funny man and the elegant man were having a conversation.

I turned to Josephine and asked, "Do you have an idea as to how much longer it's gonna take till we get to Baltimore?"

"We're fixin' to be there in about a couple hours now," she drawled. This left me very little time to ask her what I've been meaning to ask her the whole train ride.

"Oh good," I said. "If you don't mind my asking Josephine, what brings you on this train to Baltimore?"

She had taken off her bonnet as I slept and she held it in her hands on her lap. She looked down at it and said, "My husband and I live in Baltimore. I was in Chicago to visit family for a few days, but I had to leave."

I knew then that she was opening herself to trust me, so I asked, "Is everything all right between you and your husband?"

She clenched her hat and said, "He's been drinking a lot more over the past month. I caught him in our backyard fastening a noose and throwing the rope over a tree. He had a small stool with him, too, so I knew what he was about to do. I wish he never took that oath."

I got excited because now, after hours of meaningless conversation I was about to achieve what I initially planned. I would have never guessed that the person who decided to sit next to me would be such a treasure trove of information.

I had to ask, "Oath? What do you mean?"

Josephine then revealed her troubles and a few secrets of her relationship. For all she knew I was a sweet southern belle whom she would never see again. "You're a southerner, aren't you?" she asked.

I nodded and said, "I sho' am."

So she continued, "So then you know about the secessionists. My husband was a lieutenant with the Union army, but he resigned to join the secessionist cause. Have you ever heard of the Palmetto Guards?" she asked.

"Palmetto Guards? No I can't say that I have," I responded with raised eyebrows of intrigue.

"I'm not surprised, they are a secret society within the secessionists. Only a select few have entered the ranks of the guards. They usually meet at candlelit ceremonies to discuss plots in the utmost secrecy. It's all very dark and disturbing stuff, but those who are accepted into the fold are the most dangerous extremists of the secessionist cause; they are bona fide radicals. Oh, my, I have no idea why I've confided so much of my affairs with you, Amanda, but I'm glad that I got to talk to someone about this."

She smiled at me but her eyes were sad. I said to her, "I'm glad I could be of some assistance. Do you see that man over there," I pointed to Pryce. She nodded. "Before I got on the train that man was behind me and we got to talking like you and I have now. He's actually sympathetic toward our cause. I support secessionist activities, as should all southerners, but he's one of them English men. He said he was a baronet, a man of rank. I'd like for y'all to meet when we get off the train, maybe he could help your husband with his suicidal behavior?"

She looked at me with a glimmer of hope in her eyes and said, "I would like that very much."

So we began talking of lighter issues in current events and comparing Baltimore to Chicago, and the North to the South. About an hour later we pulled into the Baltimore station.

"Follow me Josephine, let's catch that Englishman," I said.

We gathered our belongings and got off the train in a single-file line. Pryce was only three people in front of us because Josephine and I got up as quickly as we could to reach him. Pryce was standing behind one of the elegant men; the funny man and the other elegant man had already exited the railcar.

When we were off the train I walked up to Pryce and said, "Excuse me sir, which way are you headed? My friend and I would like to have a word with you."

Pryce turned around and looked at us and said in a slight English accent, "A word with two lovely ladies? It would be my honor. The name is Benedict Sween." After I introduced Josephine, he invited us to dinner and we were off to the closest restaurant.

***

The Invitation

Pryce, Josephine, and I entered a restaurant to have dinner and some drinks. I did not plan on getting intoxicated and I am sure Pryce felt the same way. Our objective was to loosen up Josephine to the point where she would be willing to tell us more of the Palmetto Guards and how her husband was involved with them. I also wanted her to tell us details pertaining to secessionist plots on the railroad.

The restaurant was small and tavern-like. There was a painting of a prairie behind the bar above the bartender's head. There were several drunkards as well as women of easy virtue lining the counter of the bar. In the booths where we sat were a few couples and groups of men who were all smoking. In the back of the restaurant, I could tell there was an opium den because of the stench. This was a very low-class establishment that was poorly lit; however, it was the only place to eat close to the train station.

The booth we chose was near a window and far from all of the riff-raff. Pryce selected the quite table, which led me to believe he understood that the woman I had approached him with was well worth the time and ripe with information.

The table already had menus on it for us. When we took our seats, a man with an eye patch approached our table. He had blond hair and one blue eye. His face was covered in stubble and his nose was long and wide. The apron he wore was covered in miscellaneous residue from foods that I'm sure he'd cooked himself.

He said to us, "What'll it be folks?"

He pulled a small tablet and pencil from his pocket. Pryce ordered sausage with cabbage and rice. Josephine ordered another chicken sandwich with tea, and I ordered the flounder with beans and a cup of water.

The man nodded and said, "Comin' right up."

I had planned to begin drinking with Josephine after we ate, but just then she asked, "So y'all met before you boarded the train?"

Pryce responded "Yes ma'am, I started a conversation with the little lady here to pass the time waiting for the train. By the way," he said as he turned to me, "I didn't happen to catch your name in Chicago."

I smiled and said, "My name is Amanda Baker."

"Much obliged, Amanda Baker."

Josephine looked out of the window into the street to observe the peculiar population of Baltimore in the evening. The streets were full of gaslight, and people were still bustling about as if it were daytime. As I looked out the window with her for a few seconds, I could not help but think about the number of petty thefts that were occurring, as well as rapes and public drunkenness.

She turned around, looked at me, and said, "I just can't believe that just this mornin' we were all strangers, and now we're about to have a meal together. God moves in mysterious ways."

"Indeed he does," I said. To think that while I was on the train this morning, devising a desperate plan to make the most of a long journey amassing as much information as possible, a woman with so much useful knowledge would happen to sit next to me. Not only that, but to feel comfortable enough to share some of her woes, all pertaining to the mission, felt like divine intervention as well. I wanted her to tell Pryce of her husband and the Palmetto Guards, but I knew I could not just jump into the thick of my investigation. I would have to warm her up to Pryce.

That's when she turned to Pryce and said, "Mr. Sween..."

"Please call me Ben," Pryce interjected.

"Ben," she said, " you are an Englishman, yes?"

"Yes, ma'am," he said as he rubbed his eye with his left hand.

Josephine continued "Then why would a foreigner support southerner secessionist ideologies?"

Pryce smiled. When I saw him smile I realized that while we were on the train, he was probably deciding what to say in case someone were to ask him this very same question.

"Do you know what a baronet is Mrs. Hill? A baronet is the lowest hereditary title in the great order of British aristocracy. The only perk that separates me from a working class citizen is that I have the title of 'Sir' before my name. I love my homeland but I decided that it was time for me to start anew—meet new people, see new places, try new foods. How can one grow if one remains stagnating in the same community in which he grew up? I arrived in Chicago three years ago. I enjoyed the lifestyle of Americans but did not like the philosophies of northerners once I realized the different beliefs between northerners and southerners. While I do not approve of stagnation due to environments, I do believe in traditions. You southerners have a desire to retain your traditions, and that is an idea worth fighting for. Yes, this is not my country, but I have made this my home. I would much rather stand beside those whose, as you said, ideologies, are in correlation with my own. Does that make sense?"

After Pryce gave us his soliloquy about his made-up aspirations, I was impressed. His British accent was spot on.

Josephine responded to Pryce by saying, "I understand. You are a noble man, Mr. Benedict Sween. To leave your homeland but stand firm in your convictions regardless of the nation in which you live and call home is absolutely admirable. I see now why Amanda wanted me to meet you." She looked over at me and smiled.

It seemed as though I did not have to warm her up after all. She seemed ready and willing to tell us all about the Palmetto Guards and give us any information she had on secessionist plots. After she and Pryce spoke, the man with the eye-patch arrived at our table with our dinner. I was quite hungry because I had not eaten since the chicken sandwich on the train before I fell asleep. We all ate and had light conversation about irrelevant subject matters, as Josephine and I had done on the train.

After we ate, the man with the eye-patch collected our plates and silverware and asked if there was anything else we wanted.

"Yes, please. May I have two cups of scotch and a cup of whiskey please for this gentleman," I drawled.

Pryce looked at me and smiled. He knew what I was doing, and I also knew he was smiling because he enjoyed a drink or two of whiskey.

"My oh my, I wouldn't have taken you for a lady who would drink scotch. Thank you, the next round is on me, yes?" he said.

We all agreed and once we were served our alcohol, we drank. After two or three more drinks, I decided that it was an appropriate time to bring up what it was I had been waiting to discuss for over an hour, the Palmetto Guard.

"Do you think Ben here would be beneficial to the cause Josephine?" I asked as I sipped my cup of water.

"Oh, most definitely, I believe he is an honorable man, and I think my husband would like him very much."

"Who is your husband?" Pryce asked.

She sighed and said, "Lieutenant Hill, well, he was formerly known as that anyway. He was in the Union Army before he retired to join the secessionist cause."

Pryce raised his eyebrows and looked over at me. "He sounds like a man I would very much like to meet. Is he a recruiter of some kind or does he know of someone whom I could talk to?"

Josephine nodded and said, "He can get you in, but I don't know how well he would inspire you to lock arms with other secessionists. Lately he has been acting very depressed and angry. He drinks more often and he has become more of a recluse. He used to go to meetings all the time, but now he stays at home in his study and drinks himself into a lonely oblivion."

"What caused your husband to become so distraught?" Pryce asked.

Again Josephine sighed and asked, "Have you ever heard of the Palmetto Guard?"

This was it, the moment I had been waiting for almost all day, now we would receive crucial information that we could take back to Allan and Felton.

"No I haven't," Pryce answered.

"If you said you did," said Josephine, "I would have taken you for a liar. The Palmetto Guard is a secret society, for lack of a better term, that is a radical group of secessionists who are willing to take extreme action for the sake of the cause. You can recognize them by the gilded leaf pins they all wear on their lapels. As a matter of fact, two men that were on our train from Chicago are members of the Palmetto Guard; I saw their pins."

That's when I realized she was speaking of the two elegant men who were on the train. I had noticed their pins, but not what was on them. Those men must have been sent to watch Josephine, or maybe to escort her. Or were they sent to Chicago for the same reasons we were sent to Baltimore, to gather information.

Josephine pointed to my half-full glass of water and asked, "May I have a sip of your water Amanda?"

I slid the cup across the table. After she drank some of the water she continued on with her story. "My husband joined them a couple of months ago. They usually have ceremonies at night to discuss plots and prepare to take whatever action they deem necessary to send a message to the north that they exist and are to be taken seriously."

I could tell by the severity of Pryce's expression that he was not in character any more. It wasn't Benedict Sween who was listening to Josephine, but Pryce Lewis.

She continued, "Last week my husband came home from a meeting and he was pale-faced. I did not know what he had seen, heard, or done, nor would I ask because I knew he had taken an oath of secrecy. After a month in the Palmetto Guard he began to have his doubts and second-guess what he gotten himself into. After all of the motivational speeches he has heard and given himself, the gravity of his decisions had finally taken hold of him. Just before I left for Chicago, I caught him in our back yard with a stool and a noose. He was throwing the noose over the branch of a tree in our yard and was tying it into a knot. If I had not gone outside when I did, he would surely be dead. Oh Lord, as I sit here and talk to y'all, I can't help but worry and wonder if he is still alive. If it wasn't an ill family member that brought me there, my mind would have been set. I would have changed my plans, although he urged me to go and promised he would be here upon my return."

I looked at Pryce. He knew then why I had approached him with her. She was the key to unlocking the secessionist plots. Not only that, but if Pryce could meet her husband, then we could find out exactly what caused Josephine's husband to become suicidal. That was the mystery I wanted to solve more so than what was going to happen to some railroad. If a member of a secret sect of secessionists wants to get out so badly that he is willing to take his own life, then that sort of information is invaluable.

Pryce then asked, "Is there a way I can meet with your husband? I would love to kick him back into shape. From what I gather, becoming a member of the Palmetto Guard is an honor. An honor, that I myself, hope to one day have. If he needs a little more motivation or encouragement that what he has done and or intends to do is noble and worthy, then I would like to try and give that to him."

Josephine smiled. Pryce was a very effective undercover agent. When he spoke, if I hadn't known his true identity, I would believe in his character.

"There is a gala tomorrow night in a mansion on the hill overlooking Chesapeake Bay. My husband and I will be attending," she said. "Normally we wouldn't be invited to such a prestigious event, but because my husband is a guardsmen, we are allowed some privileges. Regardless, if y'all were to arrive with me then I know you would be welcome."

I looked at her and asked, "Your husband will not be arriving with you?"

"No," she replied. "He will be going sooner than I because there will be a gathering before the gala begins.

He will meet me at the event, so if I had not just invited y'all to join me, I would have most likely attended alone."

Pryce smacked his hand on the table and said, "Then that's it. I'm going. What about you Amanda?" He looked over at me as he put his hands behind his head.

"Of course I will go. It will be nice to have an elegant night out after traveling a whole day on that horrible train."

Josephine clapped her hands rapidly and said, "Then it is settled. I am so excited."

We all got up from the booth and made arrangements, Pryce making sure to offer to fetch us ladies properly and bring us to the mansion in style. He said he would arrive in time to have us all there by eight o'clock tomorrow night.

Chapter XII

The Plot
to Kill Lincoln

With the money that was budgeted in our contract, thanks to Mr. Bangs, Pryce and I were able to purchase the use of a very respectable carriage and extravagant clothing for the evening. I wore a purple satin dress and black heels, a scarf, and gloves. I had my hair in style and I bought a pocketbook that could hold my pistol. The shoes I wore irritated my feet because they were so straight and had yet to be broken in. I never liked buying and wearing new shoes. It took weeks before they would bend around my feet.

Pryce wore a black tuxedo with a yellow bow tie and a black top hat. When dressed elegantly, he was a very handsome man.

Josephine wore a blue gown with a pair of white shoes. Her hair was down and she did not carry a purse. When she met us she said, "I declare! Y'all look beautiful."

The night was young and the three of us became a party. When we arrived, Josephine elegantly exited the car and asked, "Are you ready to go inside?"

Pryce and I looked at each other and I replied, "Lead the way."

When we walked through the front courtyard, the first thing we saw was a fountain statue of a woman in a toga with her left breast exposed, holding a jar. The jar released water into the small pool beneath her feet. We walked along the stone path that circled around the fountain to the double doors of the grand foyer. There were white pillars surrounding the entrance to the mansion, four on each side of the doorway.

When we entered the grand hall, there was a stained-glass dome above everyone's head. There were staircases on both ends of the hall and the stairs split in two directions, which lead to the right and left side of the upper landing. Glass chandeliers holding candles illuminated the grand hall. The glass projected the candlelight, making the flames brighter and allowing the light to stretch throughout the hall.

All the men and women attending the gala wore remarkable clothing and spoke with such pretension that their conversations were lifeless and dull. There was no substance to a single word they were saying. I recall a conversation I overheard. A man was speaking to a woman in a red dress. He asked her, "Madam, why do you think that a flamboyant red dress would be suitable for tonight's festivities? This is a gala, not a masquerade my dear."

She was a rather rotund woman. Her cheeks were puffed up so much that when her mouth was closed it looked as though her mouth was full of food. "When one has the capacity to attain whatever it is that one wishes," she replied. "One holds no regard as to the occasion that one shall attend. It is a matter of economics and sincere vanity of said economics."

Never in my life have I heard such nonsense. "Sincere vanity of said economics?" How can someone truly bring oneself to waddle in the filth of her own self-righteousness, and when asked, proudly state her status is of sincere vanity? The arrogance!

I sipped my wine and turned to Pryce. He pursed his lips with his eyes closed and shook his head, indicating that he was also listening to what I was hearing. Seeing Pryce make that face, as he did when we were waiting for the train to Baltimore, made me giggle. I started to think Pryce thought the same as I did. Hurry up, Lieutenant Hill, I thought. Pryce and I could barely tolerate anymore of this pontifical pageant, also known as a gala.

Just then Josephine turned to us and asked, "Isn't this mansion just marvelous?" She was so ecstatic that she looked like a little girl who had just received a kitten. As myself, Kate Warne, I hated this gathering and I felt like I just had to leave. As Amanda Baker however, this was one of the greatest evenings of my life.

"Oh my, it absolutely is, let's go take a look around," I said as I turned to Pryce and gave him my glass of wine. "You wouldn't mind holding this for me would you Mr. Sween? Josephine and I are gonna have a little tour and have some girl talk."

Pryce smiled, because he knew my intentions, and said, "But of course, Madam."

Pryce turned and walked toward

the staircase to the upper landing. I deduced that since he knew no one here but Josephine and I, he would remove himself from the thick of the festivities and get to a vantage point, which of course would be the upper landing. From up there he could see all who entered the grand hall, and also all who occupied it. In addition, he would be able to see when we returned to the hall, and who Lieutenant Hill was, when Josephine and I returned. I knew he was expecting us to be gone long enough to enter the hall after the lieutenant had arrived and Josephine would approach and greet her husband. So we walked around the mansion's garden and admired the fountains, flowers, and the night sky. We talked about the most benign subject matters. While we spoke all I thought about was when the lieutenant would arrive and how everyone else was doing on this mission. I had not seen anyone since the meeting with Mr. Felton in Allan's office. We continued walking around the mansion's garden and other areas of the estate for about thirty more minutes until we decided it was time to enter the grand hall once more. When we arrived at the grand foyer, Josephine exclaimed, "Why, there he is, finally!" It was the lieutenant. He wore a black tuxedo and a black bow tie. His hair was curly and slicked back, making his curls appear to be waves. His mustache was thick and burly, as

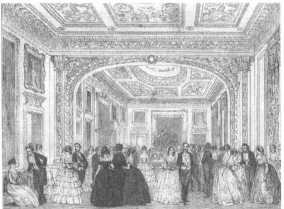

was his goatee. When Josephine approached him I looked up at the upper landing to see if Pryce was still there, but he had vanished. I walked up to Lieutenant Hill after Josephine gave him a hug and a kiss, and cordially went through the usual pleasantries of being introduced.

"Good evening, Lieutenant Hill, it is a pleasure to meet you," I said as I held out my hand. He looked at me with the concern that only a man who suffers from delusional paranoia would have. He then took my hand and kissed my glove, saying, "Not at all, Ma'am, the pleasure is indeed all mine." His breath fumed with the smell of alcohol. Josephine loved him and held him in high regards, but from what I could see, he was a drunk and a coward. I knew that I was being far too harsh, however from all the stories Josephine had told me. From the suicide attempt, the heavy drinking, and the mood swings, it was difficult for me to respect a man such as this. Especially since this was my first time meeting him and the impression I had of him from Josephine's descriptions was nothing but negative. As I was continuing my observation of the lieutenant, Pryce approached us. Josephine was startled.

"Goodness! Mr. Sween, you startled me!" she said. "This is my husband whom I've mentioned to you before." She turned to her husband and said, "Darling, this is Mr. Benedict Sween."

Pryce reached out and shook hands with the lieutenant, saying, "Just call me Ben, Sir. I've been looking forward to talking with you."

Hill gave Pryce the same drunken gaze of suspicion he'd given me and said, "Oh, is that right? Well what exactly has my charming wife said about me to you, and what do you wish to talk to me about?" I had no idea what Pryce was going to say to a drunken radical secessionist, who, by the way, was involved in a secret organization with plots so egregious that it brought him to a state of self-loathing and destruction.

Pryce then said, "You wouldn't mind if we got a drink,

walked around the mansion for a bit, and talked in privacy would you, Lieutenant?"

Hill replied, "Of course, of course. That's an English accent you got there right, boy?"

"Why yes it is, sir," Pryce replied. They both walked away after Pryce took two glasses from a server and handed one to the lieutenant. Soon they disappeared into the sea of faces, mustaches, perfumes, tuxedos, and an array of various colored dresses and gowns. After a few hours, Josephine started to wonder and worry about what had become of her husband and Pryce. We stepped outside into the main garden again and conversed as we waited. Not long after we stepped out on the back patio, Pryce and Lieutenant Hill came out of the dark night shadows with bloody clothes on their arms. Josephine stood up and dashed to her husband. She hugged him and held his arm. As she examined the lieutenant, Pryce came up to me and whispered, "Mission complete, we need to leave as soon as we can." I thought about an excuse to use for us to leave, or at least for myself. I also wondered about what had become of Allan, Hattie, and Scully. Luckily I didn't have to make an excuse because Josephine was so worried about her husband that she excused herself and her husband so she could tend to his mysterious wound. "I beg your pardon, but we must go. Between the drinking and now this wound, I don't know what's going on. I hope ya'll don't mind if we excuse ourselves."

Pryce and I agreed and showed support for her decision to take care of her husband. The Hills entered the mansion and left. That was the last time we ever heard from or saw them.

Once they disappeared Pryce said, "All right, now that they're gone, we need to go back to the train station and wait for Allan and the others." I agreed and we left the gala.

We arrived at the train station and waited for a couple of hours. I had assumed we would be taking the last train out of Baltimore to Chicago. "Do you know if they were going to be here tonight?" I asked Pryce as we sat on the bench and waited for the others.

"Yes, Allan told me he would come to the train station every night and wait for us to arrive when our mission was completed," he answered.

I was a little upset to be left in the dark as much as I was and by how Pryce seemed to have all the answers to all my questions. Why didn't Allan tell me these details? Was I really that expendable to him still? I felt as I had before when John Brown was still alive and running amok. The funny-looking man I had seen on the train approached us as we waited. Pryce stood up and shook his hand.

"Hello, Allan," I said.

The funny man smiled and replied, "You look fantastic, Ms. Warne, I truly admire that dress on you. And I gather you found me out when I boarded the train?"

I smiled and nodded. "Where are the others?" I asked.

Allan took off his hat and sat between Pryce and I and said, "They're back in Chicago. Their mission was solely to guard the train as we rode. They rode with us on separate carriages and then immediately rode back to Chicago. You and Pryce have the best methods for information gathering, so I figured I might as well have my best undercover

Men's fashion in 1850s

Abraham Lincoln made a speech at Cooper Union in New York that is largely responsible for his election.

February of 1861, President-elect Lincoln took a train from Spingfield, IL to Washington DC, where he was declared president.

agents gather intelligence while the other two guard the train. My job was to watch the two of you as well as gather my own information."

I was flattered that Allan had put me in such a vital role in this mission and that he trusted me as much as he had. We'd worked together for years, but I always doubted whether he truly trusted me, especially after our disagreement over John Brown. I'd been feeling, ever since that argument, that there was a rift between Allan and I, regardless of our romantic moments. It helped regain my confidence about his regard for me.

The final train arrived at the station. There were about fifteen of us who boarded. Allan, Pryce, and I sat in the same booth on the train. I sat next to Pryce, and Allan sat across from us. By the time we were seated it was almost midnight. I guessed we would be in Chicago by tomorrow afternoon. Once we were all settled in, it was time to fill Allan in on all the information we had collected. Not only that, but I was anxious to find out what Pryce had learned and why he had a bloody forearm. So I simply asked him, "Pryce, what happened at the gala? When you returned with the lieutenant, why did you have a bloody arm? Have you found any conspiracies we should be aware of?"

Pryce smiled and said, "I have found out everything, thanks to you."

Allan's expression changed from nonchalance to increasing curiosity. He asked, "What do you mean? How did Kate help you find out everything, as you put it?"

Pryce removed his bow tie and unbuttoned his shirt. "Josephine Hill," he said, "that's how. When we were on our way to Baltimore, I'm sure you saw Kate sitting with that woman with the bonnet right?" Allan put his hand on his chin and nodded. Pryce continued, "That was the wife of a radical secessionist who was also a lieutenant in the Union Army. We did not learn his name, so we referred to him as Mr. Hill or the Lieutenant. Anyway, during the ride to Baltimore, Kate here was softening up Mrs. Hill with conversation and camaraderie. When we got off the train in Baltimore, Kate approached me with Josephine Hill and introduced us. We had dinner together and that's when she told me what she told Kate on the train." Pryce pulled the bow tie from his collar and laid it on his lap.

Allan looked at me with a smile, as though he knew I would be able to find someone on the train or in Baltimore who had valuable information. Again, I felt I had underestimated how Allan viewed me.

Chapter XIII

Webster and Lawton

Timothy Webster was born in Newhaven, Sussex, in 1821, and when he was still young, he moved with his parents to Princeton, New Jersey. Webster joined the New York Police Department on the recommendation of Captain James Leonard, also of the NYPD.

One summer in 1853, after Webster had risen to the rank of Sergeant in charge of police patrol, Pinkerton heard about his accomplishments and was impressed. Captain Leonard, had business dealings with Pinkerton in the past and introduced Webster to Pinkerton. Pinkerton offered Webster a job with his detective agency and Webster accepted. Pinkerton gave him money to pay for his train ticket to Chicago, where he was to report to Bangs, Pinkerton's Agency Superintendent.

While undercover, Webster took the extraordinary steps to enlist in the Confederate Army, and later, with Pinkerton Detective Hattie Lawton, posed as a member of a

Timothy Webster

pro-Southern group. The two were able to report what they learned to Pinkerton.

Hattie Lewis Lawton, also a female detective, was born around 1837. Hattie, like Kate, was involved in the undercover investigation involving the confederate plot to assassinate President elect Lincoln in Baltimore. She was involved deep undercover, posing as the wife of Timothy Webster.

There was much talk among confederate troops and their officers of the planned assassination attempt on the President in Baltimore. Webster made this information known to Pinkerton. Webster continued to provide information to Pinkerton about Confederate activities and movements between 1861 and 1862 before becoming ill with inflammatory rheumatism. He became so sick he was unable to report back to Pinkerton, who became concerned and sent two of his detectives, Pryce Lewis and John Scully to find Webster. Pryce and Scully, however, were captured by the confederates. After being interrogated and threatened, Scully gave up the true identities of Webster and Lawton.

Both Lawton and Webster were arrested. Lawton was imprisoned at Castle Thunder. Though interrogated by the confederates, she never gave any information regarding her assignments or the true identity of Timothy Webster. Webster was hung as a spy on April 29, 1862. The confederates who hung Webster had failed to kill him the first time and had to drag him back up onto the gallows and hang him again until he died. Webster is said to have stated prior to the second attempt, "I suffer a double death!" Webster was then buried in Richmond and later Pinkerton had him disin-

Castle Thunder

terred and reburied in Onarga, Illinois, next to his father, Timothy Webster Sr., and his son, Timothy Webster Jr. Webster, though tortured, never admitted to his captives of his involvement as a spy.

There is some literature and information provided by various authors that Pinkerton had accidentally observed Kate and Webster kissing outside a building during one of their assignments. Pinkerton questioned her about the kiss and Kate indicated she and Webster planned to wed.

Hattie Lawton was eventually released from prison as one of four spies in a prisoner exchange. She continued under the assumed the name of Mrs. Timothy Webster. After her release she was never heard of again. As a true undercover detective, she vanished into permanent secrecy.

Chapter XIV

Guarding Lincoln

To any outsider, Kate was simply a young woman in a long dark traveling coat slowly making her way through the crowded terminal of Pennsylvania Railroad Station, guiding a tall but stooped invalid man wearing a floppy tartan hat and a shawl around his shoulders. A group of loud, inebriated southern sympathizers walked ahead of them complaining of the upcoming inauguration of "Nigger Abe." Their wisecracks set Kate's companion to spasms of laughter. Nervously, the young woman kept him moving out onto the platform.

Earlier she had affected her southern charm to demurely persuade the conductor to leave the back door of the sleeping car open so her sickly brother could climb aboard more comfortably at the rear of the train. She gave their tickets to the collector while her traveling companion settled in his compartment. As the train pulled out of the station, she joined him there. Kate and her companion

became fast friends. Humor secured their connection as they talked into the night and bellows of laughter could often be heard coming from their car.

As Kate closed the door and secured the lock, she asked Mr. Lincoln, "What do you suppose you would be doing if you had not been elected to office?"

Mr. Lincoln turned slowly around to look at her while removing the scarf they had used to disguise him. His eyes showed contemplation as well as admiration that she had dared to ask at all. "I'm not sure," he replied. "It would stand to reason that you are implying if I were to be in a totally unrelated line of employment. I do enjoy the country, although I fear I would spend most of my days fast asleep, lulled by the wind in the leaves."

Kate smiled at the thought of him lounging on a full porch, feet up, fast asleep. "So, what would engage you?"

"Comedian!" he said with a confidence and a flick of his hand in the air.

Kate outright laughed and quickly covered her mouth with a hand in apology. She had not expected that, and her response was uncontrollable.

Mr. Lincoln said, "Please don't do that."

"I am so sorry, Mr. Lincoln. I will excuse myself…"

"You will do no such thing. And what I meant was, please do not cover your laughter. It was splendid to hear and to see your face light up. I so rarely get to see anyone in good humor. Everything is all pomp and state and no one would dream of showing his or her true feelings in front of me. I wager I will see none again until I am long in the face, well, quite a bit longer than my face is already. As I said, if I were in another profession, humor would be my game. It makes a man feel good to know he may actually be good at what he would truly desire to do."

With a very big smile, Kate said, "All right, to humor

then! We shall laugh so loud tonight the cows we pass will wake and wonder what is afoot."

It was Mr. Lincoln's turn to have an unexpected laugh. Far into the night they amused each other. After he fell asleep she tiptoed into the passageway, locking the door behind her, and stood guard through the night with her revolver at hand but well hidden. Strange, she thought, how she was so natural with him. She didn't feel the need to hide anything from him, she could be the real Kate. Perhaps it was because he was not being himself today.

It would seem another wonder to Kate that she felt this was her true calling, and yet she felt she was never truly allowed to let down her guard and show her true nature, and just be Kate Warne. Was there some other profession that would allow her to be herself? One in which her inner actress could let her hair down behind the curtain? Although perhaps being on stage night after night was almost the same as being non-Kate.

Then there was the excitement of her profession. Where else could she possibly get the opportunity to have the excitement of danger so much. That was surely part of the allure to her. Acting without the danger, would that be what she wanted?

What about being a dare devil? Kate had heard of a few people, gypsies mostly, traveling around the world doing tricks and such that defied death itself…

Her thoughts rambled on into the night, rhythmically timed to the clickity-clack of their forward progression through the mysterious path that none knew about. When they arrived at the station, Allan was there to greet them. Mr. Lincoln was escorted to his destination without a single hitch.

As Kate turned to go, Mr. Lincoln reached out to her, "Kate," he said gently. "I enjoyed my time on the train

Allan Pinkerton And His Secret Service Friends

A photo of Major Allan Pinkerton with his Secret Service Department colleagues taken at Antietam, Maryland. Pinkerton is the first man from the left in the chair. For President Lincoln, Pinkerton was the head of intelligence-gathering for the Civil War. It was unofficially known as the Secret Service.

more than words can say. I would hope that we should spend more time as ourselves as often as possible."

Kate smiled slightly, ensuring that Mr. Lincoln was the only person to see it. "Mr. Lincoln, I assure you that every opportunity that presents itself to me will now be taken greedily. I thank you as well for opening my eyes to the joy of myself."

He tipped his hat to her, "Until next time Ms. Warne."

Kate made a slight and proper curtsy. "Mr. President."

Kate was just fast enough to turn around and catch the most surprised look on Allan's face. He had caught some of what had been said and now the curiosity was apparent on a face that rarely showed emotion. Allan tipped a hat to Mr. Lincoln as well and turned to escort Kate to the rooms they were holding for the night. They would return home in the morning.

Once back in their rooms, Allan made an excuse to come to Kate's room. He could stand it no longer. "What was that?" he asked.

"What was what?" Kate redirected quietly.

"What was what? You and the President of the United States is what." Allan's voice was getting a bit more brusque than it should have been. "You spend the entire evening in a rail car with the door locked, and when you depart, the two of you are both whispering your love for each other."

Kate was taken aback. Since she and Allan had kissed, they had each made an effort to stay clear of romantic encounters with each other. Now, he was obviously and very forwardly jealous. "Allan Pinkerton! If you feel that I would put myself in a compromising position with a prominent figure such as Mr. Lincoln you are much mistaken." She wasn't about to let him steal this feeling of freedom from her, the feeling of being somewhat normal. She felt like dancing.

Kate did a twirl in her dress and put on a different face when it returned to the direction of Allan. "If you would like to know, we had a splendid time just by being ourselves. Mr. Lincoln aspires to be a comedian and I will vouch for his abilities, my stomach pains from all the laughing we did. It was a most refreshing conversation, nothing more."

Allan looked a bit abashed for suggesting she would be doing anything other than her job. He realized she had recognized his jealousy immediately and quickly shut it out. "I'm sorry."

He barely had the words out before she grabbed him,

dancing to unheard music. He joined the dance, smiling, catching her joviality. "You know," he said a bit breathlessly, "I spoke to the others and I agree, our next President will surely sit at his seat entirely due to you."

"Nonsense, Mr. Pinkerton," she said coyly. "There were many involved to bring this day about." She tickled him under the chin as she danced merrily away.

Allan poured two drinks from the bar and handed her one as she danced by. "I am perfectly aware just how many people were involved, although it is due to you that we have come so far in so many ways, not just with the delivery of this precious package."

As Kate danced around, she became aware of his impatience for her to act right and listen to his compliment. He grabbed her forcefully around the waist and ceased her dance. Unfortunately, it left the two of them face to face, a bit closer than either of them had allowed since the kiss. Her breathing was heavy and in his face. Her heart raced from the dance, or was it from the moment, she could not separate the two.

The remainder of the evening went by like an explosion. Her head ached in the morning and she was unclear if it was the whiskey or the thoughts of everything that had taken place. Was she upset or happy about this event? She had been in high spirits and surely that had started everything. Was this what it was like to be Kate Warne?

Chapter XV

Without Kate

It seems a very clear path to the assumption that if Kate Warne had never been born, history would be greatly different. Certain historical episodes that define our country today would never have happened or possibly would have been delayed considerably. If Lincoln had been assassinated in Baltimore as plotted by southern secessionists we would not have had the following:

- A President who was against slavery; strong leadership during the Civil War; Lincoln's foreign policy legacy, and the Emancipation Proclamation
- The Gettysburg Address
- The Thirteenth Amendment
- The Homestead Act
- The National Banking Act
- The bill that chartered the first transcontinental railroad
- Black soldiers in the Union Army, which Lincoln admitted on January 1, 1863

The possibilities of where we would be today are endless. There have been hundreds of results of Lincoln's accomplishments alone. These would not have occurred if he lay dead at the hands of murderers in Baltimore. History, even as recent as the presidency of Barack Obama, would have been altered. President Obama would not have been able to state during his campaign that we look to Lincoln as a model. We would not have had the many famous quotes of Abraham Lincoln to guide us.

The criminal element of the day would have not missed Kate Warne if she had not been born, but Chicago itself may not have risen to be the successful metropolis of today. It might have been overrun and controlled by those she put behind bars. She changed so many things that it is unimaginable to have been without her.

On January 28, 1868, the first American female detective, Kate Warne, died at age 38. She was at the Pinkerton's residence at 94 Washington Street, Chicago, Illinois, when she succumbed to congestive lung failure as a result of pneumonia. Kate had been at Pinkerton's side for twelve

years, and he was justly at her bedside when she passed.

Having had no other relatives, like so many detectives of her time, Kate is buried in the Pinkerton family plot in Graceland Cemetery in Chicago along with other detectives from the Pinkerton Agency. Being an undercover detective during the Civil War was extremely dangerous. Many undercover detectives and spies on both sides ended up in prisons or killed, and it is often difficult to be sure of their final resting places.

Kate's reputation as an honest and dedicated undercover operative for the Pinkerton Agency led the way to a female detective unit within the agency, which she managed. Other women were able to show their worth and contribute, as Kate did, to a previously all-male profession. Kate was a first, in the nineteenth century when employment for women was scarce, particularly in this male-dominated position.

Word spread and soon police departments all over America recognized the value of female law enforcement officers and began hiring and training them. Criminals who could pick out undercover officers a mile away were thrown a curve ball, in the shape of a pretty face and the fanciful relations of the female gender. Still today, criminals are caught off guard by well-trained undercover female detectives.

Women across the entire United States in law enforcement, be it a police or sheriff's department, state, federal, or private investigation agency owe a debt to Kate as a result of the work she did for Pinkerton's Detective Agency. As the Wright Brothers were to flight, Kate Warne was to law enforcement.

Like the saying goes, "behind every great man is a women." The woman behind Allan Pinkerton changed the world.

A Remembrance

Author Roger Wright wrote a beautiful remembrance of Kate Warne. If you would like to read more writings by Roger, he also published 'Finding Work When There Are No Jobs' and co-authored 'I Am Your Neighbor: Voices of a Chicago Food Pantry'.

The writing that follows is the entire piece he wrote in honor of Ms. Warne, posted on October 13, 2013 and can be seen online at:

http://chicagoguy14.wordpress.com/2013/10/13/kate-warne-never-sleeps/

Kate Warne was the nation's first female detective. She died at 38 of congestion of the lungs and is buried in the Pinkerton family plot in Graceland Cemetery Chicago.

Every October she gets a visitor who comes to say "Thank you." I hope you enjoy it as much as I did. Thank you Roger Wright.

"I'm Kate.

My last name? The gravestone says Warn. No "e" at the end. But I have had lots of names. I can tell you that when the tall, thin man dressed in black with the sad, haunted eyes comes to visit, comes here to Graceland Cemetery in Chicago each October, he calls me Kate.

I rest now and forever near Mr. Pinkerton. And it should be that way. Without Mr. Pinkerton, I would never have met the tall sad man. Without Pinkerton, they would never have said, "Kay Warne, she never sleeps."

After I came to Graceland, people wrote, "Kay Warne, the first lady detective." I never understood why being first was important. What was important, was that I was good.

I was only 23 when I first stepped into Mr. Pinkerton's Detective Office in Chicago. But I hadn't been a little girl in a very long time. My husband had passed. So it was just me, and I needed a job.

I knew I could find out things about people that no one else could. I knew I could find secrets. So, at ten o'clock in the morning of August 23rd, 1856, Mr. Pinkerton gave me a job. I was a detective now.

Wives and girlfriends would tell me the things they would never tell a man. Like Mr. Maroney, in Montgomery Alabama. He embezzled $50,000 from his company, the Adams express company. And I got the true story from his wife. The true story and $39,515 back for the company.

Mr. Pinkerton was pleased. He said I was one of the best he'd ever known.

Bank robbers and killers. I found their secrets. I stopped their evil deeds. And when I walk these golden brown grounds of autumn, I am pleased with my life's work. My years were *few. I passed soon after the War Between the States. I was 38. But I am pleased with my life's work.*

In October, I remember my best work; it's October when the sad eyed man who had just been elected to be President comes back to visit me.

My work with the President-elect began with the tips we got of the secessionist plots in Baltimore. The cry to crack open the Union was echoing across the land in those times, splitting up what America had become.

But it was what I found out next that could have ripped open the very fabric of these United States and left it to bleed and die.

There was a plot to kill the new President-elect as he changed trains in Baltimore. There was a one-mile carriage ride between the two train stations. The secessionists would cause a diversion. The President elect guards would respond to the diversion. And a crowd would swarm the unprotected carriage and kill the soon-to-be President. He would never complete the trip from his home in Springfield, Illinois to the muddy streets of Washington.

But with Mr. Pinkerton by my side, I was able to make the case for what I had found. I convinced the President-elect that there really was danger. So after the President-elect's last speech of the evening in Harrisburg, Pennsylvania, we changed the travel schedule for the last leg of the trip into Washington D.C. Mr. Pinkerton

had the telegraph lines interrupted so no one would know of the change. And then we dressed the President-elect in the suit of a traveling common man. We put a soft felt hat on his head and told him to carry a shawl as if he was an invalid. When he got on his new train I cried out a greeting as if he were a long lost brother. And throughout that long dark night, as the train pulled into an empty Baltimore at 3:30 a.m., as opposed to the much earlier hour that had been planned, I sat next to him. Kept him safe.

I got him to the White House alive. Because throughout that night I never slept.

He was inaugurated. Became the President. And he saved the union. He kept alive the great American dream.

This is why he comes to see me each October. He comes to say thanks.

President Abraham Lincoln. The tall, thin man with the haunted sad eyes. He comes here to Graceland. Offers me his arm. And we walk. Through the orange, red and brown scattered leaves of time. He is known by so many as the centuries pass, this President Abraham Lincoln. And few remember my name.

But he remembers. He comes each October and we walk the grounds of Graceland together.

And when I look up at those sad eyes and see him looking at me under an October moon, I can actually see those haunted eyes, just for a moment, fill with joy."

***

It should be noted that due to the findings of prior researcher, Jane Singer, the true name of Kate Warne has come into question. "Kate had many aliases which included Kate Warn, Kate Warne, Kate Warner, Mrs. Barley, Mrs. Cherry, Mrs. Warren, and Angie M. Warren." In the log book at Graceland Cemetery there is an entry in handwriting on 1/30/1868, which lists an Angie M. Warren. Signed by the undertaker, a Jas. W. Wright. Angie M. Warren is later recorded as Kate Warn. (Singer, Jane)

"Kate's grave location is next to the memorial marker of Timothy Webster. Timothy's remains lie with Pinkerton's family in Onarga, Illinois." (Singer, Jane)

It was also found that Erin, New York at the time of Warne's birth was actually in Tioga County, not Chemung County. (Singer, Jane)

Singer also stated that Kate Warne is actually Angie M. (Mahala), and recorded at the cemetery as Angie M. Warren. Singer has also indicated that Kate is actually Angie M. Warn, Mrs. Warren, and Angie M. Warren.

Source:

www.janesinger.com/.../10/HOW-TO-Catch-ASPY-1.pdf Retrieved 2/6/2014

As most all of the histories written around the Pinkerton Agency and any mention of Kate Warne, these writings had to employ fiction within. She was not properly mentioned in history or written about enough for true histories of her life to be transcribed in total. She, as many women of her time, was not glorified as she deserved.

As mentioned and well put:

"Some people leave only their bones, though bones too make history when someone notices." and "Well-Behaved Women Seldom Make History"—Laurel Thatcher Ulrich

References

Murphy, Clayton,(2014) Town of Erin, New York, Historian

Hibler, Neil S. (1995) *The Care and Feeding of Undercover Agents*

Farkas, G.M. (1986) *Stress in undercover policing*

Hibler, N.S. (1978) *The psychological autopsy*

Reiser, M., & Sokol, R. (1971) *Training of police sergeants in early warning signs of emotional upset*

Kurke, Martin & Scrivner,Ellen M. (1995) *Police Psychology*

Lerner, Eric (2008) *Pinkerton's Secrets*

Stashower, Daniel (2013) *The Hour of Peril, The Secret Plot to Murder Lincoln Before the Civil War*

Pinkerton, Allan (1884) *Thirty Years A Detective*

Ulrich, Laurel Thatcher., *Well-Behaved Women Seldom Make History*

Singer, Jane, *How-to-Catch-A-Spy*

www.janesinger.com/.../10/HOW-TO-CATCH-A-SPY-1.pdf Retrieved 2/6/2014

Chicago Guy's Blog (2012) *Kate-Warne-Never Sleeps*

www.chicagoguy14.wordpress.com/2013/10/13   Retrieved 02/06/2014

Turner, Thomas P.(1863) *Rules and Regulations of the C.S. Military Prisons.*

From the Author

Thank you for reading. Kate Warne was of great interest to me because I was a law enforcement officer for twenty years. I also see a lot of her fortitude in all my family members. As I delved for information and came up quite a bit empty handed, my publisher and I decided we would need to fill in a lot of the blanks.

With the help of works from other authors as well as the great writing by my team at MotherSpider.com I feel you have not only an enjoyable read, but also one that is filled with many facts about the time period and as much information that could be found about Ms. Warne.

I wish there was more about her. She truly should be celebrated as one of the great ladies of firsts. I can only presume, due to her occupation, that everything was kept hidden.

Please leave a review at Amazon, any other site you purchased this book through, or on the MotherSpider. com website. We would love to know what you thought.

- John Derrig

John Derrig

John was born in Montour Falls, NY and grew up in Watkins Glen, NY, about 15 miles from Erin, NY, the probable birth place of Kate Warne.

He started a law enforcement career walking a patrol beat, then driving a patrol vehicle, and later was awarded the department's gold shield as a Detective. He worked undercover as a police detective making controlled purchases of drugs, and once people found out his undercover capacity, continued as a detective utilizing a wire on informants in the Ontario County, NY area. He received two departmental medals, one was for undercover drug investigations and the other for the arrest of a individual armed with a rifle atop a 30 ft. grain tower, waiting to ambush a Sheriff's Deputy, who had arrested him earlier in the week for DWI.

After retiring from law enforcement in 1998, John returned to college and received his BS degree, MS degree and Ph.D (ABD). Currently, he works with exceptional fellow employees for the Florida Dept. of Economic Opportunity, as a State of Florida Fraud Investigator.

John is married to Doris Derrig who is in the same line of work. She owns a Private Investigation Agency called Precaution Private Investigations, out of Cape Coral, Florida. Both his son and daughter are police officers as well as his son-in-law.

He and his wife have two beautiful granddaughters, and a dog named Chaos.

51414965R00095

Made in the USA
Columbia, SC
17 February 2019